SKY BANDITS

At 0630 hours, four hours after leaving Noemfoor, 44 B-24s were droning over the Tomini Gulf in the Celebes before crossing the island's northwest isthmus and then heading over Makassar Strait to Balikpapan. But at 0635 hours, waist gunner Sam Leffort on Col. Bob Burnham's lead B-24 spotted a swarm of planes to the south—the 24 Japanese fighters from Kendari under Commander Iwami.

Moments later, the Japanese pilots roared into the American bombers, spitting chattering 7.7 machine gun fire and whooshing 20mm shells at the fat bellied Liberators. American gunners, meanwhile, swung turret, belly, and waist guns at the Japanese planes, unleashing streams of .50 caliber machine gun fire. The sky trembled from the heavy exchange that echoed across the gulf like a staccato of thunder.

The first diamond of four Liberators caught withering machine gun fire as the Oscars made several passes in two plane attacks. About 20 7.7mm hits tattooed the wing and fuselage of Burnham's lead plane, forcing him and his co-pilot to cover instinctively. The hits opened holes in the fuselage and cold, heavy blasts rushed inside the plane and struck the waist gunners like multiple streams of arctic air. . . .

THE SURVIVALIST SERIES
by Jerry Ahern

THE DEADLY SKIES

BY
LAWRENCE CORTESI

ZEBRA BOOKS
KENSINGTON PUBLISHING CORP.

ZEBRA BOOKS

are published by

KENSINGTON PUBLISHING CORP.
475 Park Avenue South
New York, N.Y. 10016

SECOND PRINTING MAY 1987
Printed in the United States of America

THE DEADLY SKIES

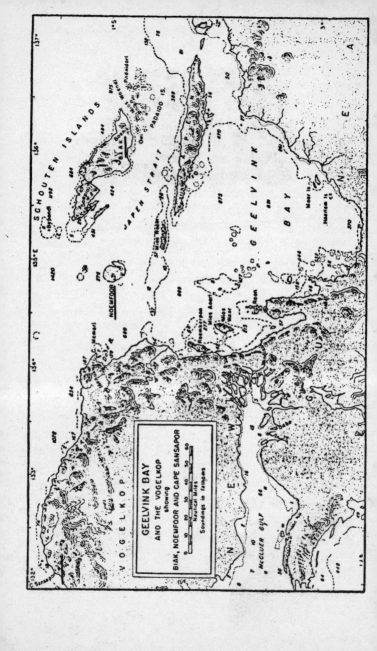

GEELVINK BAY
AND THE VOGELKOP
showing
BIAK, NOEMFOOR AND CAPE SANSAPOR

Nautical Miles
Soundings in fathoms

Chapter One

By September of 1944 one thing was certain: Gen. Douglas MacArthur would invade the Philippines. The CinC of the Southwest Pacific Allied Forces had spent a year and a half in conquering eastern New Guinea, the Solomons, the Bismarck Archipelago, and Neomfoor and Biak in western New Guinea. Meanwhile, Adm. Chester Nimitz had spent the same period moving westward across the Pacific, taking the Gilberts, Marshalls, the Marianas, Paulus, and a host of other Pacific island chains. Further, the Americans had reduced the Japanese to impotency at Truk and Rabaul.

In a final step before the Philippines, MacArthur had invaded and occupied the island of Morotai, only 400 miles from Mindanao and halfway between western New Guinea and the Philippines. However, before MacArthur landed in the Philippines, he would ask his airmen to fly on one of the most astonishing and dangerous series of air attacks ever conducted in the Pacific war.

On 19 September 1944, Col. Tom Musgrave, commander of the U.S. Fifth Heavy Bomb Group, got a memo from FEAF (Far East Air Forces) to report to Hollandia for a conference at SWPA headquarters. Musgrave was bewildered by the summons because field officers below brigadier never got called to VIP conferences. His Fifth Group and the 307th Group, also a B-24 unit, had recently moved to Kornasoren Drome on Noemfoor Island near the western end of Dutch New Guinea and he had expected to begin air missions to the Philippines. But, flight orders usually filtered down to him from 13th Air Force headquarters, so Musgrave could not understand why he had been called to Hollandia.

The day after the summons, Tom Musgrave arrived at SWPA headquarters from Noemfoor. He could only conclude that MacArthur wanted to discuss the role of his B-24s in an upcoming invasion of the Philippines. He expected to find other SWPA brass here: George Kenney, CinC of FEAF; Gen. Walter Krueger, CinC of the 6th Army; Adm. Daniel Barbey, commander of the 7th Fleet; and perhaps lower brigadiers like Gen. Ennis Whitehead of 5th Air Force and Gen. St. Clair Streett of the 13th Air Force.

However, Musgrave was surprised when he arrived at SWPA headquarters. Except for Gen. Richard Sutherland, the SWPA chief of staff, all those in attendance were airmen: Kenney, Whitehead, Streett, and Gen. Paul Wurtsmith of FEAF Fighter Command. Also here were Gen. Millard Harmon of the FEAF Aviation Engineers and other heavy bomb group colonels: Bob Burnham of the 307th, Ed Scott of the 90th, Jim Potty of the 43rd, and Richard Robinson of the 22nd.

Why were only airmen here? Where were the generals of the U.S. ground forces and the admirals of the U.S. Navy who would play a major role in the Philippine Islands invasion?

At 1300 hours, after a noon time meal, MacArthur called his meeting to order. Some of the FEAF colonels felt uneasy, awed in the presence of MacArthur, especially when they looked at the circle of gleaming asterisks on his shoulders, the rank of a five star general. Most of these air commanders, including Musgrave, had never even seen MacArthur, much less attended one of his VIP meetings. But, despite the general's usual staid countenance, MacArthur eased the tension with a small grin and friendly gesture.

"We didn't bring you here to eat you up, so please remain at ease."

However, Musgrave and the other colonels noticed a hard, sober look on General Kenney's face. The FEAF commander seemed piqued by the meeting, as though he did not want to be here at all. Kenney's countenance surprised Musgrave because the colonel had always known him as a man with a bubbling outgoing character, a man always saturated with enthusiasm. Further, General Whitehead and General Streett also appeared somber.

MacArthur cocked his head, and an aide lowered a huge map on the wall behind the SWPA CinC. The map portrayed the entire Western Pacific, including New Guinea, the East Indies, and the Philippines.

"Gentlemen," MacArthur began, "we're here to discuss a series of vital air raids, perhaps the most ambitious of the Pacific war." He referred to his map. "You can see where we've come so far. We now have heavy bombers at Kornasoren Drome on Noemfoor and at Biak in Geelvink Bay in the northwest area of New Guinea. We don't know when Morotai will be ready for heavy bombers, but General Harmon hopes to have the Warma and Pitoe airfields ready by mid-October."

The group air commanders only listened.

"I guess it's no secret that we will shortly invade the Philippines," MacArthur continued. "The purpose of occupying Morotai was to give us an advanced staging area for assaults on those islands. But," the SWPA CinC gestured, "the meeting here today has nothing to do directly with the Philippine invasion."

Col. Tom Musgrave frowned and he then found the courage to question the five star general. "What do you have in mind, sir?"

"We know a couple of things from air reconnaissance over the Philippines and from partisan reports out of those islands," MacArthur said. "The Japanese fully expect an invasion and they're doing all they can to defend the islands. They've brought in hundreds of aircraft for their 6th Base Air Force, they've brought in thousands of troops with plenty of armor, and they've been assembling heavy warships and aircraft carriers at Formosa and Borneo. We can expect the enemy to resist in the Philippines with everything they can muster."

Col. Bob Burnham, commander of the 307th Bomb Group, half scowled to himself. He, like everyone here, knew that MacArthur had engaged in a recent verbal war with Admiral Nimitz, the Pacific Fleet commander, over strategy. Nimitz had wanted to bypass the Philippines and invade Formosa, thus cutting off the Japanese and allowing them to wither away as they had withered in New Britain, Wewak, Sarmi, and possibly the East Indies with the invasion of Morotai. But, MacArthur had insisted on his "I shall return to the Philippines" strategy, a campaign that would cost the Americans thousands of lives.

Burnham considered the invasion of the Philippines dumb, since MacArthur himself had proven the worth of his own island hopping manuevers which had won the United States substantial gains on the road to Japan with minimal losses.

The U.S. now had far superior resources in men, planes, and ships. If they seized Formosa and cut off the Philippines, the huge U.S. navy and hordes of FEAF aircraft could easily maroon the Japanese in those islands as the Americans had isolated other Japanese forces in the Southwest and Central Pacific. But Burnham did not express his opinions out loud. He only looked again at the glum faces of Kenney, Whitehead, and Streett.

"Now," MacArthur gestured again, "we must do something that will minimize Japanese resistance in the Philippines. We can't stop them from bringing in planes, men, and ships from throughout Southeast Asia and their home islands. But we all recognize an essential factor for their military operations — fuel. Like us, the Japanese need oil to fly their planes, sail their ships, and move their troops. Without fuel, mobility is impossible. In Europe, the destruction of Hitler's refineries and oil sources is the principal reason for the Allied advance across France. Without fuel, the Germans cannot fly their planes and run their tanks. I propose that we also deny fuel to the Japanese, so they cannot effectively resist us in the Philippines."

"How can we do that, sir?" Colonel Musgrave asked.

MacArthur grinned again and slapped a finger on

the map—Borneo. "Here, Balikpapan. The Japanese are almost totally dependent on the oil they get from the Indies to run their war machine. The enemy has established a unique system in Borneo for fuel allocations. They don't carry the crude oil back to Japan, especially since our submarines have been quite successful of late in sinking tankers. Instead, they've improvised and expanded their refineries at Brunei and Balikpapan to process the crude. Then, tankers carry the fuel to their airbases and ground installations, while warships and supply ships come into Brunei or Balikpapan to refuel. Suppose we denied the Japanese the use of their important refineries?"

"General, sir," Burnham suddenly hissed, "our B-24s can fly a long way, but we'd need so much gasoline to reach the refineries at Balikpapan that we couldn't carry much of a bomb load. As for Brunei, we couldn't possibly reach there even if we stripped our planes of all armament and guns."

"It is true that we can't reach Brunei—not yet," MacArthur conceded. "But, I believe we can attack the Balikpapan refineries with substantial bomb loads. We have all of our heavy bombers now on Biak and Noemfoor. So, they're less than 1100 miles from Balikpapan. You'll recall that the 380th Bomb Group struck the same refineries about a year ago, flying out of Darwin, a distance of 1200 miles one way. I believe, with proper planning, we can carry maximum bomb loads from our current airbases."

"Sir," Tom Musgrave now spoke. "the 380th did a courageous thing, but they really didn't do that much damage, and they took serious losses."

"I realize that," MacArthur nodded, "but we've

planned a different strategy this time. We intend to make a series of assaults on Balikpapan, repeated air strikes over a two week period to make certain we've destroyed the entire oil complex. I'll ask General Kenney to explain." He gestured toward the FEAF commander. "George?"

The air commander nodded and then the diminutive Kenney rose to his feet. He shuffled through some papers in front of him. And if he lacked enthusiasm, Kenney certainly showed no hesitation in outlining the plan.

"We do have some excellent photos of the Balikpapan refineries," the FEAF commander began. "They were taken by long range PBY reconnaissance planes on August 3rd, 4th, and 5th. There are several facets to this oil target. First, the Japanese have a lubricating plant, a paraffin plant, and a distillery. They also have the huge Pandansari Refinery, a new and modern plant that's essential for the distillation of aviation gasoline. Then there's the cracking plant, a central structure in the area, on which they depend for gasoline refinery. And finally, there's the Edeleanu plant which the enemy needs to produce sulfuric acid for the solvent treatment of aviation gasoline."

"We tried to get B-29s to do the job," General Whitehead suddenly spoke, "but without success. We wanted to borrow two very heavy bomb groups from the XX Bomber Command in China or the XXI Bomber Command in the Pacific, but the Army Air Force refused to lend us the units. General Arnold (CinC of USAAF) told us the B-29 commands could not afford to release any of their Superforts, so we'll need to do the job with our B-24s."

"We do know that the attack on Balikpapan by the 380th Group a year ago did have some effect," Kenney said. "After the raid, the Japanese were short of aviation fuel for their air units at Amboina and Wewak, and even at Paulus and Truk. So, as General MacArthur pointed out, if we thoroughly knock out Balikpapan with a series of raids, the Japanese will surely suffer a severe handicap in their defense of the Philippines. A reduction of refined black oil at Balikpapan would also disrupt enemy operations in other forward areas."

"Well, sir," Colonel Burnham said, "we know that a 1,000 mile flight in itself is not a problem, but with all that extra necessary fuel, I'm not sure we could carry much of a bomb load."

"We have data from MAAF in the ETO concerning the B-24 attacks on the Ploesti air fields," General Kenney said. "We can take advantage of their experience since their raid on the Romanian oil fields also required their B-24s to fly more than 1,000 miles one way. Following MAAF's suggestion, we'll make our first two attacks with 250 pound bombs, with each Liberator carrying eight of them instead of the usual 12 to 16. That would enable you to carry plenty of fuel. The bombardiers will spread these 250 pounders all over the Balikpapan complex to fracture oil containers and to ignite fires."

"On succeeding raids," General Streett now spoke, "all B-24s will carry 500 or even 1,000 pound bombs to destroy the installations."

"Yes sir," Colonel Burnham said.

Kenney shuffled through more papers and then continued. "We intend to make five attacks on the

Balikpapan oil complex, spacing the missions two or three days apart. These missions will be primarily a 13th Air Force show with the 5th Air Force groups as support."

Streett then looked at some papers and spoke again. "Our plan is to send the 307th, 5th, and 90th Groups on the first mission, with a target date of 29 September. The 13th Air Force heavy groups will make the second attack on 2 October, also with 250 pound bombs. On subsequent raids, the heavies of the 5th Air Force will join the heavies of the 13th Air Force to flatten the complex with heavy bombs. We plan to conduct these later raids on 5, 7, and 10 October respectively, so the bomber crews will have at least a full day's rest before going out again."

"Sir," Colonel Burnham asked, "what about escort?"

General Streett frowned before he spoke once more. "General Kenney, General Whitehead, General Wurtsmith, and I have discussed this aspect of the plan quite thoroughly and we've determined that we simply cannot supply fighters. Balikpapan is too far away. The nearest fighter units are at Sansapor, and that's 936 miles one way from Balikpapan."

"Even if the fighter strips at Morotai are ready by the end of the month," General Wurtsmith now spoke, "it wouldn't do any good. The Morotai fields are 845 miles from Balikpapan, still too far for P-37s and P-38s."

"You are saying, sir," Tom Musgrave asked uneasily, "that we'll have to make this long flight through enemy territory without fighter escorts?"

"I'm afraid so, Colonel," General Streett nodded.

"But the Japanese have several big airfields between here and Borneo?"

"If you keep a tight formation, and if you keep your gunners alert, you should not have much difficulty," Kenney said. "Our reconnaissance shows that the Japanese do not have many planes on these fields between Sansapor and Balikpapan. They do have a fighter unit at Amboina and fighter squadrons at Kendari and Manado in the Celebes. They also have air units at Batjoli in the Halmaheras. However, so far as we can tell, they have no combat planes in Balikpapan itself."

"We'll be conducting heavy air strikes against these airfields over the next ten days," Whitehead spoke again, "and we expect to have them effectively neutralized by the time we launch our first strike against Balikpapan. At worst, you'll only run into light to moderate AA fire, so fighter escorts will not really be necessary. Actually, boredom will likely be your biggest problem since you'll be airborne for at least 12 hours."

"If any aircraft get shot up too badly," General Streett said, "the pilots can head for Morotai. General Harmon is sure he'll have at least emergency runways there by the end of the month."

"We've been working very hard on the Morotai airstrips," General Harmon said. "We've been delayed because of heavy rains, but I'm sure the Warma strip will be ready for emergency landings."

"Yes sir," Musgrave said.

"I must add," MacArthur spoke again, "that the enemy's Netherlands East Indies oil installations are the finest and most decisive set of targets for bombing

14

that you'll find anywhere in the world. You and your airmen have spent two years in the Southwest Pacific bombing nothing but one jungle target after another, or maybe Japanese ships once in a while. But this time, you'll be hitting something big, lucrative, and extremely important. You'll know what you've bombed and you'll know the results. For the first time, you'll be on a target that parallels the kinds of targets they have in Europe."

MacArthur sighed and then continued. "I'll leave the details of this operation in the hands of General Kenney. He'll work out a strategy with Generals Whitehead and Streett, who will in turn devise the flight orders for the group commanders."

"Sir," Colonel Burnham said, "you mentioned Morotai as a possible emergency landing field. What happens if one of our planes needs to ditch in the sea?"

"I was coming to that," Kenney said, shuffling through more papers on the table. "We've got a squadron of PBYs stationed in Sansapor and we'll have another PBY unit at Morotai. The Catalina commanders have your air route going and returning, with the times and dates of your missions. They'll cover the seas all day to pick up anyone who's been forced to ditch. We'll also have a squadron of submarines from the Freemantle Submarine Fleet. I believe these subs include the *Mingo, Jacks, Paddie, Flying Fish, Guavina,* and *Bashaw.* They'll be on patrol along the flight routes. Three subs will operate in Makassar Strait between Balikpapan and the Celebes, and the other four will be in the Molucca Sea between the Celebes and Halmahera. We will establish a code to call the submarines or the PBYs to give your location in the event you go down."

"That would help, sir," Colonel Burnham said.

"If there are no more questions," General MacArthur said, "I suggest you return to your units and prepare for both the preliminary air missions on the Japanese airfields and the main attacks on Balikpapan. I've asked General Kenney to launch the series of air strikes at once against the Celebes, Halmahera, and Ceram enemy airfields. It is my understanding that General Kenney will use the 5th Air Force to assault the Ceram and New Guinea fields, while the 13th Air Force will attack the Celebes and Halmahera fields."

"Even many of the medium and light bomber groups will hit these fields," General Kenney said. "By the time we launch the first strike on Balikpapan, there shouldn't be much air opposition. Anyway, we're pretty sure that the Japanese have been sending all of their replacement aircraft to their Philippines bases, with very little going to the Indies."

"I believe," General MacArthur said, "that this series of raids against the enemy airfields will convince the Japanese that we're clearing the way for the invasion of the Philippines and not opening an air route into the Balikpapan oil complex."

The group commanders did not answer.

When the conference ended, MacArthur allowed the colonels to quarter themselves at SWPA headquarters for the rest of the day. Still, they were quite busy because after the evening meal, General Streett called Musgrave and Burnham into conference to discuss plans for the 13th Air Force attacks on the

Celebes and Halmahera airfields. Similarly, General Whitehead called Colonels Scott, Pottys, and Robinson into conference to discuss the 5th Air Force raids on Amboina in Ceram Island and Babo in New Guinea. The group commanders left Hollandia in the morning and returned to their bases at Noemfoor and Biak.

When Col. Tom Musgrave arrived in Noemfoor, he met with his operations officer, Capt. William Stewart.

"Well, Colonel?" Stewart asked anxiously. "What was the VIP conference all about; are they laying plans for air support on the Philippines invasion?" Before Musgrave answered, the captain shook his head, frowned, and continued. "Christ, Mindanao's a long way off. I don't know how we're going to hit Jap bases there unless we stage out of Morotai."

"The conference had nothing to do with the Philippines," Musgrave said.

The 5th Bomb Group operations officer looked puzzled.

"Our targets are the oil refineries on Balikpapan. They want us to hit them in several raids so the Japanese won't have oil to feed their ships, planes, and army in the Philippines."

"Good Christ," Stewart huffed. "that place is over 1,000 miles away and the Japs have airbases all along the way."

"Beginning tomorrow, the 13th and 5th Air Forces will launch a series of strikes against these airfields to neutralize them and clear the air route for Balikpapan. The brass says it will work, but Kenney and

Streett didn't seem too enthusiastic about the whole thing."

"This'll be murder," the 5th Group captain shook his head. "We'll be down and sinking all over the Celebes and Molucca Seas. They talk so much about those Ploesti raids in Europe; goddamn it, this'll be worse."

"MacArthur thinks the Japs will interpret the preliminary raids as an effort to knock out their air power for our Philippines invasions. They won't expect us to hit Balikpapan."

"Maybe," Stewart conceded. "We only made one raid on that place a year ago and I suppose the Nips figure we'd have gone there again long before this if we intended to hit that oil complex."

"That seems to be everybody's opinion," Musgrave said. Then he sighed. "Well, let's take stock on available aircraft, crews, and armament. We're going to have a busy couple of weeks."

"Yes sir," Captain Stewart said.

But the Americans were naive indeed to believe the enemy considered Balikpapan a target to be ignored. The Japanese knew very well that fuel would be vital in the expected battle for the Philippines, and they realized that the Allies knew that Balikpapan was a prime source for much of this petroleum. Imperial Japanese Headquarters had every intention of protecting this oil producing center.

Chapter Two

Among all of Japan's conquered peoples in the Far East, the Indonesians of the Netherlands East Indies gave the Japanese the least problems. Punjab Sukarno, who became Independent Indonesia's first president after World War II, had been active in the Independence movement against Holland since the 1930s. He and his nationalist followers had continually complained of Dutch rule and he welcomed the Japanese who had ousted the Dutch from the East Indies. Gen. Soemu Anami, who commanded the Japanese 2nd Area Forces in the Indies, had promised Sukarno and other nationalists that Japan would give Indonesia its independence after the war. In fact, Anami had quickly released from custody such fiery nationalists as Sutome Hatta and Thramrin Sjahrir who had been imprisoned by the Dutch for their anti-colonial activities.

The Indonesians, in fact, had even raised a volunteer army to aid the Japanese in the Pacific war against imperialist Britain and Holland. Gen. Kasman Songodimeajo, a native Indonesian and a devout Muslim, had numbered among his native troops 70 battalion commanders, 200 company commanders, 60 lieutenants, and 2,000 non-coms. Many of these troops were stationed in Borneo where Japanese Gen. Sosho Ichabangese maintained the headquarters of his

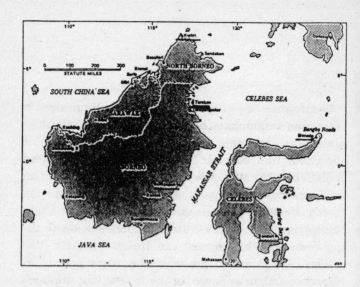

Makassar Base Force occupation troops at Balik-papan.

Ichabangese had nurtured an excellent paternal relationship with the Indonesians, but he did have advantages. First, because the area profited from a wealthy oil industry, local residents enjoyed a high economic status compared to most people in the Far East. The Japanese paid oil workers well as long as they kept gasoline continually flowing out of the refineries. Further, the local civilians found their lives less restricted than other people in Japanese conquered territories. For Imperial Japan, as long as the vital gasoline and fuel came from the refineries, the Japanese pretty much left the Indonesians alone.

Imperial Headquarters had issued General

Ichabangese a simple order: "We must have fuel. Do whatever is necessary to keep the refineries flowing at full capacity." Because the Indonesians worked, Ichabangese showed them great tolerance so the occupying Japanese and Balikpapan residents got along well.

The general's second advantage was beautiful Balikpapan itself. The city offered ideal circumstances for Japanese troops stationed here. Westerners had always called Manila in the Philippines the Pearl of the Orient, but not enough of them had ever visited Balikpapan on the eastern coast of Borneo. The thriving city of 80,000 was populated by perhaps the most handsome people in the Far East. These Malaysians were light skinned, well proportioned, neatly dressed, and almost immaculately clean.

The city's friendly, pretty women were a boon to Nippon soldiers as was the city's bustling business district. Cinemas, restaurants, public swimming pools, and cabarets gave the Makassar Base Force troops plenty of gratifying diversions. General Ichabangese and his soldiers wallowed in true luxury compared to weary Nippon combat troops who for two years had been fighting the losing battles in the Pacific under miserable, half starved, disease ridden conditions in the jungles of the Solomons, New Britain, and New Guinea.

Balikpapan's features and climate far surpassed that of any urban area in the Dutch East Indies. From anywhere in the busy downtown streets to the fine residential suburbs one could see the surrounding mountains and the steep, terraced rice fields. Throughout the city, palm and bamboo trees lined

21

the streets, interspersed with other dazzling trees: flames of the forest, city-of-gold, on African tulip. Tropical gardens in the parks flourished with flowers of every description and along the coast the soft, pleasant breezes floated across the relatively calm Makassar Strait to cool the face and body in this tropical town with an 80° norm temperature, 100 inch rainfall annually, and high humidity.

General Ichabangese maintained his own headquarters in a former Dutch colonial administration building which sat on a rise outside of the city. From his terrace he could see not only the city and countryside, but also the rows of barracks which housed his troops, the barracks which housed Korean coolie workers, and the small houses of Indonesian civilians who worked at the refinery. He could also see the bustling oil complex itself, where wisps of smoke, from pure white to dark gray, curled upward from the humming plants. He could also see the rising mountains to the west and north.

For nearly two years, General Ichabangese had lived in this uninterrupted paradise with untroubled serenity while other Japanese commanders had been fighting the terrible, deterioriating struggle throughout the Southwest and Central Pacific. Imperial Headquarters had left him alone as long as the refineries pumped fuel and fed the Japanese war machine. But in September of 1944, even Ichabangese grew uneasy. The Allied tentacles had been coming ever closer to his elegant haven and now, with the occupation of Morotai by the Americans, even the Makassar Base Force commander realized that the powerful American air force might come within bombing range of his beloved Balikpapan.

Ichabangese confirmed his suspicions when, on the very next day after the American Morotai invasion, he received a communication from Gen. Soemu Anami, CinC of the 2nd Area Forces with headquarters at Kudat, Borneo. Anami informed Ichabangese that he would hold a conference with 2nd Area Forces commanders at Balikpapan, whose accommodations at the Hotel Duba were among the best in the Far East. And even though Ichabangese was not a combat commander, this meeting concerned him so the conference would be held at the Makassar Base Force headquarters. Anami suggested that the general's chief of staff, Col. Koichi Kichi, also attend the meeting.

Over the next two days, General Anami and other 2nd Area Forces commanders arrived in Balikpapan: Adm. Mitsuo Fuchida, CinC of the 4th Air Fleet with headquarters in Singapore, Adm. Kuso Morita of the 9th Fleet, and Capt. Zenji Orita, commander of the 1st Submarine Squadron.

After the assembled Japanese officers ate breakfast on the morning of 18 September, they sat about an oval table at the Makassar Base Headquarter's operations room. When they were settled, General Anami rose to his feet and shuffled through some papers he had brought with him from his own headquarters in Kudat.

"I have called this conference," the 2nd Area Forces CinC began," because it is now evident that the enemy intends to invade the Philippines. We do not know when or where, but he has obviously seized Morotai and Peleliu to use these islands as forward staging bases for such an invasion. General Yamashita, who commands our forces in the Philippines, has worked in concert with Admiral Toyoda of the Combined Fleet and General Tominga of the 6th Base Air Force. They have drawn up plans for the defense of the Philippines and their efforts require us to help them."

"And what will be our part, Honorable Anami?" Ichabangese asked.

"With the enemy's occupation of Morotai," Anami said, "we can assume that he will attempt a blockade of the sea lanes between the East Indies and the Philippines. That in itself cannot harm Yamashita since all reinforcements in men, planes, and arms will come from Formosa or the home islands. But," he gestured, "General Yamashita and Admiral Toyoda will need the oil that comes from the Borneo refineries at Brunei and Balikpapan." He looked at Fuchida. "You will agree, Admiral, that we will need aviation gasoline for the many aircraft that are now arriving daily in the Philippines for the 6th Base Air Force?"

"Indeed," Admiral Fuchida answered. "Without fuel which comes from Balikpapan, General Tominga cannot possibly fully operate the many air units that are now coming under his command in the Philippines. In fact, his needs will be at a maximum in this obvious upcoming battle."

General Anami nodded and then looked at Ichabangese. "You can see, Shosho, that a defense of these refineries at Balikpapan is vital. We would be naive indeed if we thought the Americans had no intention of making air attacks on the oil complex. Our enemy knows as well as we do that fuel and gasoline will be a prime requisite to successfully defend the Philippines.

And now, with their advanced air bases in Geelvink Bay and possible new bases in Morotai, they are only 1,000 miles from Balikpapan, well within range of their heavy Liberator bombers. We must take measures to defend the refineries against such contingencies."

"I can assure you, Honorable Anami," Ichabangese said, "that the Makassar Base Force will do all that is necessary to cooperate."

Anami nodded. "As a start, I suggest that you order a blackout every night in Balikpapan and the surrounding area, beginning tonight. The Americans have been conducting more air attacks at night in recent months and we cannot rule out such night air attacks here. They have rightly concluded that our fighter units are not trained for night time interception as are the German fighter units, and their bombers will not be harassed by fighter planes at night."

"If they cannot see their targets at night," Admiral Fuchida said, "they cannot damage such targets."

"I understand," Ichabangese said.

The suggestion of a blackout in his darling city depressed the Makassar Base Force commander. The order would remind him, his troops, and the Indonesians that the war had caught up to them. A blackout would mean no more pleasant strolls on the neon lighted streets, no more relaxing night drives in the countryside with a pretty woman, and no more exciting parties in his palatial quarters. But, worst of all, the blackout would clearly hint that Japan's enemy was encroaching ever further westward and this knowledge would erode the pleasantries and gaiety that had so long prevailed in Balikpapan.

"General," Anami again addressed the Makassar Base Force commander, "you will henceforth take all precautions to guard the various plants of the refinery."

"But the local Malaysians have been most cooperative."

"Still," Anami said, "there are always those few who favor our enemies. We are, after all, occupiers of their country. These Malaysians may conclude that if the Americans come here with their bombers, they may soon arrive with their invasion forces. We have found that our conquered peoples have a tendency to change allegiance quickly to the winning side. Besides, the Indonesians hold no animosity against the Americans as they do against the British and Dutch. Further, many of these Indonesians know that the United States has promised independence to the Philippines after the war and the Americans would also favor such independence to the Netherlands East Indies."

"Perhaps you are right, Honorable Anami."

The 2nd Area Forces CinC nodded. "You must guard the refinery complex carefully against saboteurs and malcontents. You must also build defenses along the shorelines. While we expect the enemy's next offensive to come in the Philippines, one never knows. They may also attempt to seize Balikpapan for the Americans now have the resources to carry out multiple invasions."

"Yes, Honorable Anami," Ichabangese said.

"I will draw up a plan to guard the refineries and to build shoreline defenses as soon as possible,

26

Honorable Ichabangese," Colonel Kichi suddenly spoke.

"Very good, Colonel," the general nodded.

Anami shuttled his glance among his officers and then spoke to Mitsuo Fuchida. "Admiral, while I recognize that the bulk of our efforts must be devoted to the Philippines, we also have needs in the Indies, particularly to protect Balikpapan against air attacks. It is our responsibility to furnish air strength with the 7th Air Division and 23rd Air Flotilla which are under your command."

"I understand," Fuchida said. "I have already discussed such measures with Colonel Matsumae and Captain Sonokawa. We have planned to defend the Indies with three hundred aircraft, mostly fighters."

"Very good," Anami said.

Fuchida rose from his chair and referred to the sheet in front of him before he spoke again. "We will shortly have twenty-four full squadrons in the 4th Air Fleet command, of which twenty will be fighters. The 23rd Air Flotilla now has two Kokutais of Mitsubishi (Zero) and Nakajima (Oscar) fighter planes based in Kendari in the Celebes and we will bring in a Kokutai of Kawasaki (Tony) fighter planes to this base. They will have a mixed Kokutai of fighters and bombers at Bitjoli in the Halmaheras and a Sentai of fighters at Amboina on Ceram Island. The 7th Air Division has two squadrons at Manado in the Celebes and a squadron in New Guinea at Babo. All total, this amounts to more than two hundred aircraft. We also intend to send two squadrons of fighter planes to Balikpapan itself. This will include the 7th Air Division's 381st Sentai under the capable Lt. Satoshi

Anabuki and the 20th Navy Kokutai under the renowned Lt. Commander Nobuo Fujita. Another squadron of fighters will remain at Kudat and we can draw from this unit if these reserves are needed."

"Very good," General Ichabangese said.

"I must tell you, General," Fuchida gestured, "that I have examined the airfields here at Balikpapan and I must say that they are completely inadequate. The runways need smoothing, the drainage must be improved, and revetment areas must be constructed to shelter aircraft. I must also have housing for Lieutenant Anabuki, Lt. Commander Fujita, and their pilots."

"Yes, of course," the Makassar Base Force commander said.

"You will put your troops to work at once to improve the airfields," General Anami pointed to General Ichabangese.

Ichabangese grinned sheepishly. "The fault is mine. We have found no need to maintain the fields for combat operations during these many months. Only transport and supply aircraft have occasionally flown into Balikpapan."

"You are fortunate," Fuchida scowled. "Other base commanders have been continually harassed by enemy air assaults, and their troops have often worked around the clock to repair and service fields so that combat air units can operate against the growing strength of our enemy." The 4th Air Fleet commander obviously felt a mixture of envy and contempt for Ichabangese, who had lived a quiet life of tranquil self-indulgence during these hard months of war.

28

The Makassar Base Force commander did not answer Fuchida. He only lowered his head in embarrassment.

"I will want to move the 381st and 20th air units to Balikpapan as soon as possible," Fuchida said. "I shall remain here for the next few days to oversee the work on the airfields. The improvements must be completed at once and they must meet our specifications."

"Of course, Admiral," Ichabangese said. He did not like the idea of the 4th Air Fleet commander remaining in Balikpapan, but he could hardly refuse.

"Admiral Fuchida has offered excellent suggestions for an air defense of the refineries," Anami said, "and I am grateful to him. But we must have as many resources as possible to defend Balikpapan, so that we may destroy enemy bomber formations even before they reach here. I have invited Admiral Morita of the 9th Fleet to this conference. He and I have held meetings in Davao and he has drawn up a plan for an early warning system against such enemy bombers. Admiral?"

Morita nodded and then rose from his chair. "As you know the 9th Fleet has a limited number of vessels, mostly subchasers and gunboats. Admiral Toyoda has commandeered almost every ship from desroyer size up for the Sho strategy in Philippine waters. Still, we do have the 1st Submarine Squadron assigned to us. Capt. Zenji Orita, who leads this squadron, has discussed strategy with me at length."

The admiral now walked to the wall and pointed to the huge map of Indonesia. "We know that enemy air strikes will be launched from their bases at Noemfoor and Biak in Geelvink Bay where the Americans have

29

now stationed their heavy bombers. There is also the possibility that they might launch strikes from Morotai as soon as they have completed airfield improvements there. We are therefore setting up a series of submarine patrols along two possible air routes that would be used by Americans air formations in combat flights to the oil complex at Balikpapan."

Morita then gestured to Captain Orita who rose from his chair and went to the map himself. The submarine commander placed a finger on a stretch of sea between the Halmaheras and New Guinea. "We will have two I-boats patrolling Djailalo Passage as our first warning measure against enemy air units that come from Geelvink Bay. If the Yankee aircraft successfully avoid these submarines, we will have three more I-boats patrolling the Molucca Sea between Molucca Passage to the north and Butung Island to the south. Such I-boats can alert the airbase units in the Halmaheras and Celebes and these units can then alert their radar teams to expect such approaching enemy aircraft. Four R-boats will patrol Makassar Strait between Borneo and the Celebes. I am certain that American air formations cannot possibly avoid all of these submarine patrols."

"Should the enemy launch an air strike," Admiral Fuchida said, "he will need to be airborne at least five or six hours to reach Balikpapan. Thus we will have ample time to detect them and intercept them."

Fuchida paused and then continued: "To summarize, we will have the 383rd Army Sentai at Babo and the 384th Sentai at Amboina. The army 19th Squadron under the capable Lt. Kuniyoshi Tanaka will be at Bitjoli in the Halmaheras, the 22nd Navy

Kokutai under Cmdr. Joyotara Iwami at Kendari in the Celebes and the 382nd Sentai under Lt. Masayuki Nakase at Manado, also in the Celebes. Finally, the 381st Army Sentai and the 20th Navy Kokutai will be here in Balikpapan. I therefore concur —the Americans cannot reach the oil complex before they are intercepted."

"You are to be congratulated for your excellent planning for an air defense, Admiral," General Ichabangese said.

The 4th Air Fleet commander grinned at the Makassar Base Force commander. "I must emphasize again, General, that we will need accommodations here at Balikpapan for the squadrons of army and navy aircraft. It is important that we improve your airfields quickly to station at least one hundred combat fighter planes, their pilots, and their ground crews."

One hundred! Ichabangese was shocked. War had indeed come to his pleasant city on the shore of eastern Borneo. "We will cooperate fully, Admiral."

"Good," Fuchida nodded.

"There is one more point," General Anami spoke again, "and that is the anti-aircraft defenses for the refinery complex. I have ordered the 246th Anti-aircraft Battalion to this area at once. Maj. Toshiro Magari, who commands this unit is one of the best officers in the Imperial Army. He has worked in the Philippines to set up anti-aircraft defenses, and he had been responsible for such defenses in the Solomons and in New Britian. Now he will bring his experience and leadership to Balikpapan."

"His gunners are the best," Captain Orita said. "I

have watched them in action during the New Britian campaign."

"He will have about forty 75mm and 90mm guns which he will place strategically about Balikpapan for maximum effect against enemy bombers," Anami said. "He should be arriving at Balikpapan with his guns and troops within a week or ten days. General Ichabangese, you will give Major Magari whatever freedom he needs to set up defenses wherever he deems necessary."

"Colonel Kichi and I will fully cooperate, I assure you."

"Now, are there any more questions concerning our defensive measures for the Balikpapan refineries?" Anami asked. When no one answered, the 2nd Area Forces CinC nodded and then continued. "If there is nothing more, we will end this conference. Admiral Morita and I will return to our headquarters in Kudat. Admiral Fuchida will remain here to oversee the work on the airfields so the base can accommodate the two squadrons of air combat units. General Ichabangese, you will prepare dock crews to receive Major Magari and his troops, guns, and supplies. You will also prepare quarters for these anti-aircraft gunners as well as the combat airmen who will be arriving here."

"Honorable Anami," Ichabangese said, "I do not have facilities for these increased troops. Our barracks are already filled with our own troops and the coolie laborers. Will the 2nd Area Forces supply bivouac tents in which these new arrivals can live?"

General Anami's neck reddened. He leaned over the table and glowered at Ichabangese. "Do you dare to suggest that these fighting men house themselves under primitive field conditions, while your soldiers continue to live in comfortable quarters as they have for two years? These airmen and anti-aircraft gunners have fought long and hard in our bitter struggle against the enemy. They have often been deprived of food, medicine, and the most simple luxury. The gunners of the 246th Battalion spent countless sleepless nights for more than a year in their harsh battles against American air attacks. Do you propose that they continue to live with such deprivations?"

"I only meant—"

"I know what you meant," Anami barked angrily. "Do you have tents here in Balikpapan?"

Ichabangese looked at Koichi Kichi who nodded and then looked at the 2nd Area Force commander. "We do have tents, Honorable Anami," Kichi said, "but they have been stored in warehouses for many months since we had no need for them."

"Well, Colonel," Anami sneered, "you have need for them now. Your soldiers will vacate as many barracks as necessary to house the pilots and ground crews of the 4th Air Fleet as well as the combat gunners of the 246th Anti-aircraft Battalion. Your displaced troops will themselves set up accommodations in tents. I also expect the soldiers stationed here to become service troops for the combat forces. Admiral Fuchida and Major Magari are to be given free rein and your troops will serve them however they see fit. I do not know what else your soldiers are good for after growing soft and lazy during these many months of idleness."

Ichabangese only squirmed in his chair.

"I fear, General," Anami sneered again at the Makassar Base Force commander, "that the life of comfort so long enjoyed by the officers and men of your command has now come to an end."

Neither General Ichabangese nor Colonel Kichi answered.

"Have I made myself clear, Shosho?" Anami barked.

"Yes, Honorable Anami," Ichabangese answered. "We will carry out your wishes without fail."

Thus did an abrupt change come to the Japanese troops who had so long enjoyed fat cat duty at Balikpapan. They would be reduced to lackeys who would engage in the unaccustomed activity of serving combat troops and airmen, and living under drastically reduced conditions.

But the continued flow of fuel and gasoline from Balikpapan obviously depended on combat forces, and General Anami wanted combat leaders like Fuchida and Magari to take the reins. Although Ichabangese would remain in charge of operations at Balikpapan, the 2nd Area Forces commander wanted tested fighting men to hold as much responsibility as possible, rather than leaving such responsibility to men who had not fired a gun against Japan's enemies. Nor was Anami about to allow these combat officers and men to live under harsh conditions, while the Makassar Base Force soldiers continued to live their pleasant, confortable lives.

Chapter Three

Two days after the meeting at Hollandia, General Kenney appointed Gen. St. Clair Streett, the 13th Air Force commander, as the OTC for the Balikpapan air campaign. Then, on 25 September, Streett met with group commanders from FEAF bomber and fighter groups at ADVON 13th Air Force headquarters on Noemfoor Island. His aides passed out copies of FO 316 before the general addressed those present.

"We'll spend the next three days hitting the major Japanese bases between here and Balikpapan. These airfields must be reduced as much as possible to minimize interception during the refinery raids." He pulled down a large map and then used a pointer before he continued. "These are the enemy bases where recon pilots have sighted substantial Japanese aircraft, particularly fighter planes: Zeros at Babo right here in New Guinea, at least a squadron of fighters at Amboina in Ceram, and a squadron at Bitjoli in the Halmaheras. Our medium and light bombers will hit these bases."

The officers listened.

"Two major enemy bases are here at Kendari and Manado in the Celebes," Streett continued, "but we don't think there's anything at Balikpapan or Tarakan itself. We only saw a few transport planes on Manggar Field and a few cargo planes at Samarinda Drome in Balikpapan. Obviously, the enemy does not expect us

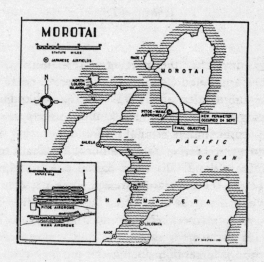

to fly that far west. However, there are considerable ships in the harbor at both Balikpapan and Tarakan. 5th Air Force heavies will hit this shipping."

"What about the 13th groups, sir?" Bob Burnham asked.

"The 307th Group will hit Manado; the 5th Group will hit Kendari. The 90th Group from the 5th Air Force will hit the shipping at Tarakan and the B-24s of the 43rd Group will hit the shipping at Balikpapan. Medium and light bombers from the 345th, 38th, 417th, and 3rd Groups will hit Bitjoli, Amboina, and Babo."

"What about fighter cover?"

"The medium and light bomber groups will have cover," Streett said, "but we can't furnish cover for the heavies because we have no fighter planes within range of the Celebes or Borneo. Even if the engineers get a fighter strip ready at Morotai to stage fighters, the P-38s and P-47s will still be too far away from these islands."

Col. Burnham looked gloomy. He did not relish a nearly 1100 mile flight one way without escort. There would be a serious danger from several enemy bases during the long, tedious flight to Balikpapan. He only hoped that preliminary attacks on these Japanese airfields would indeed clear the way.

On the morning of 26 September, Burnham briefed his pilots of the 307th Group for the raid on Manado, the target for the Long Rangers. "We'll attack in three plane waves. The 372nd Squadron will hit the runway. I'll take in the 372nd myself and Major Reese will take in the other squadrons to hit the runway with 1000 pound demolition bombs."

"What about fighter cover?" Major Clifford Reese asked.

"Manado is too far away, even from Morotai," Burnham answered. "But, light and medium bombers will go off earlier to hit the enemy bases at Babo, Bitjoli, and Amboina. That should minimize fighter interception from these fields."

However, the assurance did not bring much relief to the 307th crews. They would be flying about 800 miles one way, and the Japanese could still mount aircraft from dozens of their smaller bases in the East Indies.

By 0700 hours, Burnham was in his lead B-24 at the head of the Kornasoren runway on Noemfoor Island, waiting for the green light from the control tower. The four engines of his big Liberator screamed with a deafening din as the B-24s props emitted a wild slip stream to the rear. On the taxiway, like monstrous spiders plodding toward an unsuspecting prey, 26 more B-24s lumbered toward the runway to take off. Finally, the green light blinked from the control tower and Burnham released the brake. The plane lurched forward, picked up speed, and roared down the runway. The heavy bomber rolled for more than a mile before the plane hoisted itself skyward.

Behind Burnham, in A/C 587, Lt. Ron Covington watched the lead Liberator rise into the air before the green light blinked again. Then Covington released his brakes and the B-24 tore down the runway. From the right waist, Sgt. Joe Black watched the plane rush toward the end of the strip. The gunner knew that B-24s sometimes failed to get off before they reached the end of the runway. However, the plane rose upward long before reaching the end of the strip.

Next came A/C 570, piloted by Lt. Don Forke, who also waited for the green light. When he raced down the runway, Gunner Ralph O'Brien, from the bubble turret position, studied the flat landscape of Noemfoor Island or the line of B-24s behind him which also lumbered over the taxi strip toward the runway. When he felt the feathery feeling, he relaxed. The plane had risen from the strip.

Behind these first three Liberators came six more B-24s of the 372nd Squadron. The Liberators then circled in the sky before they settled into a pattern of 3 plane Vs. In Burnham's lead plane, Sgt. Ed. Anderson, the nose gunner, peered down at Noemfoor to watch other 307th Group planes still taking off. In the waist position, Gunner Sam Leffort stared out the window at the hanging B-24 on the left point of the lead V. Sgt. Leffort jerked when Colonel Burnham cried over the intercom.

"All stations, report!"

"Waist guns okay," Sgt. Sam Lefford said.

"Turret guns in order."

"Nose guns fine," Sgt. Ed Anderson said.

"Instruments working," Co-pilot Joe Redrick said.

Burnham also got positive responses from his tail gunner, belly gunner, the navigator, the bombardier, the engineer, and the radio operator-waist gunner.

Soon, the nine B-24s of the 372nd Squadron and nine Liberators of the 370th Squadron had joined with the 372nd Squadron to jell into formation. Then the three squadrons of Long Rangers settled into an easterly course. Col. Bob Burnham called Clifford Reese.

"Major, everything okay?"

"I've checked with everybody, Colonel. No problem."

"Remember, our 372nd Squadron goes in first to hit parked aircraft. You come in next to hit the runway, and the 373rd follows to hit the same Manado runways."

"Yes sir," Reese answered.

Before the 307th Group Liberators had disappeared into the western sky, the heavy bombers of the 5th Group, 26 of them, had reached the head of the Kornasoren runway. In the lead A/C 595 B-24, Col. Tom Musgrave waited for the green light. In the cramped tail section, Gunner Jim Shaw peered at the rocking B-24 behind him that waited to take its place for take off. Shaw felt a little depressed as he always did just before take-off because he had never become accustomed to the hours of flight in these cramped quarters, and even the relatively short seven or eight hour flight today did not help.

In the nose, Gunner Harold Trout peered about him, also waiting for the go ahead. When the green light blinked, Trout felt the B-24 lurch forward and pick up speed. He watched the long runway disappearing under him and he squirmed uneasily as the seconds passed while the B-24 still clung to the ground. However, on this relatively short 800 mile flight, the aircraft was not overly loaded and the B-24 became airborne after using little more than three fourths of the mile and a half long runway.

In the ball turret, Sgt. Marv Anderson watched the ground below diminish into a miniature landscape as the B-24 rose higher into the sky. Like Shaw in the tail, Anderson also felt cramped in his belly position. Further, the sergeant did not like this position. Although he always had an excellent view of a target below, he rarely saw enemy interceptors which came from the laterals, and he never saw Japanese planes that came from above. Shaw swung his twin fifties to release some of his stiffness.

When Musgrave was airborne, Lt. Jom Russell, behind the 5th Bomb Group leader, roared his own B-24 down the runway and rose upward, much to the relief of turret gunner Joe Tribble and waist gunners Charlie Smith and Hal Phillips. The three gunners aboard this A/C 572 were on their twenty-first mission, and this one to Kendari meant they would be airborne for perhaps eight hours. But worse, the three Bomber Baron airmen knew that Kendari was a major

Japanese airbase in the East Indies, and they expected to meet a sky full of enemy interceptors along with heavy ack ack fire. The gunners did not appreciate that kind of opposition without fighter plane escorts.

After Russell took off, Lt. Ken Guthiel sped his B-24 *Blackjack* down the Kornasoren runway and surprisingly, the plane got airborne long before he reached the far end of the airstrip. Top gunner Chuck Lee and waist gunner Wes Barker did not even have time to worry about getting off. They felt relieved, for they knew that most aircraft mishaps occurred during take-offs.

For another ten minutes, the B-24s of the 5th Bomb Group roared down the runway and took off. Finally, the 26 Bomber Baron Liberators had jelled into formation and droned and westward at 10,000 feet. Then, Col. Tom Musgrave called his squadron leaders. "Everything okay?"

"Okay in the 72nd," Major Jim Pierce answered.

"No problem in the 22nd, Colonel."

"All in order in the 31st, sir."

"Tell your crews to relax," Musgrave said. "We aren't likely to meet any kind of enemy opposition until we're well into Djailalo Passage."

"What about interceptors from Amboina or Babo?" Major Pierce asked.

"The mediums and lights took off about an hour ago," Musgrave said. "They should be keeping the Nips well occupied at those bases as well as at the enemy base at Bitjoli."

Then, the 5th Group Liberators flew almost directly east. They would cross the Vogelkop Peninsula at the western head of huge New Guinea, then cross Djailalo

Strait, the southern tip of the Halmaheras, and then Molucca Sea to their Kendari target in the Celebes.

On the island of Biak, just east of Noemfoor in Geelvink Bay, and also in the Schouten Islands group, 23 Liberators of the 90th Bomb Group had reached the head of Mokmer Drome runway. In the lead A/C 367 of the Jolly Rogers' 320th Squadron, Maj. Vernon Ekstrand was first to speed down the runway. Among his crew, including co-pilot Ed Cromwell, navigator Will Abeil, and waist gunners Al Tulley and Frank Gutierre, the men had remained silent during take off. They would be flying nearly 1200 miles on this mission against shipping at Tarakan, Borneo. They had struck targets in this area before, as well as along the shipping lanes between Borneo and the Philippines. But they had never liked the flight; it was too long, too tiresome, and too deep into enemy territory; and their planes were too heavily loaded with bombs and fuel. The U.S. airmen suspected that Bitjoli in the Halmaheras and Manado in the Celebes were jammed with interceptors which would jump them as they skirted these islands and droned over the Celebes Sea.

Ekstrand's crew knew the FEAF medium and light bombers had gone out earlier to hit these airbases enroute to Tarakan, but these assurances had not eased their trepidation. American air groups had hit these targets before but the attacks had not stopped Japanese fighter planes from intercepting them over the Celebes Sea. The gunners on Ekstrand's plane checked and rechecked their guns and ammo to make certain their weapons were in order and they had plenty of .50 caliber belts.

As soon as Ekstrand was airborne, Lt. Frank Mann roared down the runway in his *Mann's Morons* Liberator. Co-pilot Al Rehm looked at the instrument panel and then at the long runway ahead. He did not relax until the plane hoisted itself skyward. Only yesterday, Rehm had seen a Liberator run off the runway, slam into some trees, and then catch fire. Half of the crew on the ill-fated plane had died in the flames.

When the twelve B-24s of the Jolly Rogers' 320th Squadron were airborne, the eleven Liberators of the 319th Squadron came to the head of the runway. Ground crews watched Maj. Charles Briggs, the squadron leader, race over the runway in his *Phyllis J. of Worcester*. In the co-pilot's seat, Lt. Hank Pennington stiffened as hard as concrete as the big bomber neared the end of the long runway before the Liberator finally took off only a few yards from the end of the strip. The co-pilot sighed in relief as the plane rose upward.

Pennington had been Briggs' co-pilot on his last dozen missions and he had developed great faith in the 319th Squadron commander. Only two weeks ago, the lieutenant had pinned Briggs' gold leaf on his shoulder when the squadron leader made major. Still, Pennington never got over his fear of taking off in a heavily loaded bomber.

Navigator Tom Glassman as well as gunners Steve Novak and Harry Clay felt equally tense until they too felt themselves rise into the air.

The ground crews at Biak watched until the last of the 23 Jolly Roger Liberators had disappeared into the western sky. Then they shuffled away, broke up into small groups, and returned to their campsites. The

90th Group personnel moved away in silence. They would not see their combat crews for at least twelve or fourteen hours and they doubted that all 23 aircraft would return.

At Owi Field, also in the Schouten Islands group, 16 Liberators of the 43rd Bomb Group had also taken off at 0700 hours on this 26 September morning. These airmen would also make a flight of more than 1100 miles to hit shipping in Balikpapan Harbor. The Ken's Men of the 43rd would get a close up look at the city and its oil facilities. The Americans were after shipping today, but photographers would take photos to get an up to the minute look at the Balikpapan complex. The 43rd combat crews expected to find supply ships that might be unloading provisions, men, and armor as well as oil tankers that were loading fuel and gasoline for transport to Japanese army, air, and naval units in the Philippines.

The Ken's Men hoped that other FEAF air units would neutralize the Japanese bases at Ceram, Halmahera, and the Celebes, and perhaps the 43rd would not meet enemy planes along the lengthy route to Balikpapan.

By 0800 hours, the air bases of the U.S. heavy bomb groups in the Schouten Islands had grown quiet. The big Liberators were gone, and ground crews of the 307th, 5th, 90th, and 43rd Groups could do nothing but wait restlessly all day until their Long Rangers, Bomber Barons, Jolly Rogers, and Ken's Men returned to base late this evening. As always, they prayed that every plane and every man returned unscathed, but experience had told them that some planes might not return. Since moving to the

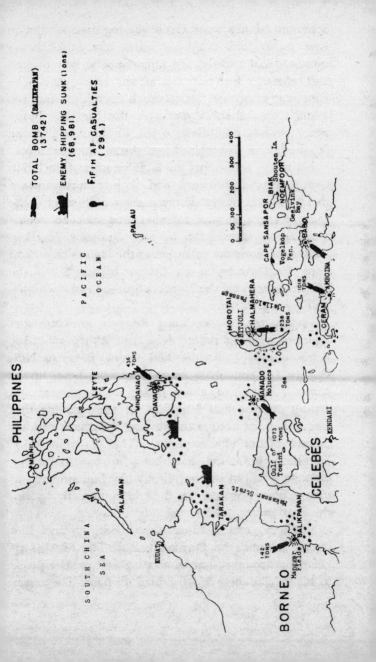

PHILIPPINES

TOTAL BOMB (BALIKPAPAN) (3742)

ENEMY SHIPPING SUNK (tons) (68,981)

Fifth AF CASUALTIES (294)

MANILA

LEYTE

PALAWAN

SOUTH CHINA SEA

PACIFIC OCEAN

PALAU

MINDANAO   436 TONS
DAVAO

BORNEO

KUDAT

TARAKAN

Makassar Strait

BALIKPAPAN   142 TONS
Manggar Field

CELEBES

Gulf of Tomini   1073 TONS

MANADO   Molucca Sea

KENDARI

MOROTAI
BITJOLI
HALMAHERA
DJAILOLO   238 TONS

CAPE SANSAPOR
Vogelkop Pen.

BIAK   Shouten Is.
NOEMFOOR   Geelvink Bay

SABO

1018 TONS

CERAM   AMBOINA

0   50 100   200   300   400

Schouten Islands bases and beginning their attacks on East Indies and Phillipine bases, the FEAF heavy bombers had aroused the Japanese who now offered stiff resistance with anti-aircraft and interceptors. The American crews had not met such opposition since the assaults on Rabaul a year ago. But the East Indies were the last roadblock to the Philippines and the Japanese were determined to maintain this roadblock.

For nearly four hours the 27 Liberators of the 307th Group droned westward and slightly north toward their Manado target. Every passing mile relaxed the Long Ranger airmen for they had met no enemy interceptors from Babo on New Guinea's Vogelkop Peninsula, none out of Bitjoli in the Halmaheras, and none from Amboina on Ceram Island. Soon, the 307th was crossing the Molucca Sea and came within a half hour of target.

Fortunately for the Long Rangers, medium and light bombers had indeed done their job this morning. A-20s out of Hollandia had struck Babo in New Guinea at about 0700 hours, punching holes in the runway, destroying about a half dozen planes, and setting afire several buildings. If the light bomber assault did not destroy the airbase, the attack had left behind plenty of destruction. The Japanese 383rd Squadron personnel had been so busy repairing damage and putting out fires, they had no time to mount planes against the B-24 formations flying into the East Indies.

Similarly, two B-25 medium bomb groups had struck Amboina on Cerman Island. The FEAF Mitchells had come in low on strafing and parafrag runs to hit the Japanese 384th Squadron base. The attack had chopped up the runway and destroyed five Oscars and three Betty bombers. The Japanese became completely preoccupied in repairing the field, snuffing out fires, and clearing debris. They found no time to send out interceptors against the Liberators.

And finally, FEAF medium bombers had struck Bitjoli in the Halmaheras with 500 pound demo bombs which left an array of craters on the main runway, set aflame several Vals and Zeros, and smashed four service buildings. Lt. Cmdr. Kuniyoshi Tanaka, CO of the 19th Kokutai, needed to devote all efforts to repairs and fire fighting. Tanaka simply ignored reports from coast watchers who had seen the formations of B-24s droning over Djailalo Passage.

But in Manado, Lt. Nasayuki Nakase, commander of the 7th Air Division's 382nd Sentai, got off 20 Zero interceptors before the B-24s of the 307th Group reached target. Nakase led his airmen swiftly eastward to meet the Long Rangers before the Liberators reached Manado. Col. Bob Burnham, in the lead bomber, saw the dots in the distance and he quickly called his crews.

"Bandits! Bandits at 12 o'clock high! All gunners, man your stations; man your stations!"

Sgt. Sam Leffort cursed. Only yesterday, 24 September, PBY scout plane crews had reported a mere six enemy fighters at Manado. The reports had obviously been inaccurate for now a swarm of Zekes was coming after the Liberators. Leffort checked the triggers of his waist guns and then waited. However, before he saw any enemy planes, the gunner heard a fleeting whine and then a chatter of machine gun fire that punched several holes in the fuselage. The

47

sergeant winced instinctively and then looked out of his waist porthole. However, he saw nothing. The attacking Zero was long gone.

In the nose of this lead 307th aircraft, Gunner Ed Anderson saw clearly the oncoming Japanese planes and he fired furiously at the whining Zekes with his twin fifties, while 7.7 fire from enemy planes missed the Liberator.

During a five minute period, the Zeros made several passes at the big American bombers. However, the U.S. pilots held their tight formations, where six gunners on each B-24 offered plenty of firepower against the arcing, diving, zooming Zeros. The Long Ranger gunners downed two of the Japanese planes and damaged several more, without losing any of their own heavy bombers. Soon, the Japanese pilots backed off and made only half hearted further attacks against the heavily armed Liberators, never coming closer than 800 yards before arcing away. Lt. Nakase scolded his pilots and urged them to press their attacks. But, the Japanese airmen had become squeamish after their losses and damage.

However, the 307th Group still faced a serious challenge. As the B-24s crossed the coastline and droned toward Manado airfield, heavy AA fire spewed up at the American bombers. Now the U.S. air crews ogled at the puffs of ack ack that burst all about their formation. Some of the Liberators caught hits and some crew members were killed or wounded from flak shrapnel. But none of the B-24s went down.

Finally, the Vs of heavy bombers soared over the airfield, with the first wave at 13,000 feet, the second at 14,200 feet, and the 3rd at 13,700. In Colonel

48

Burnham's lead aircraft, Bombardier Wes Brown ignored the bursts of flak about him and peered carefully through his Norden bomb sight. Finally, he released his pathfinder flare and then cried into his radio phone.

"Bombs away!"

Then, a sextet of 500 pound demolition bombs sailed down on Manado and exploded in a string of blasts along the buildings and aircraft adjacent to the airstrip. A confetti of heavy bombs from other 372nd Squadron B-24s also erupted in a staccato of explosions against aircraft and several buildings about the Manado runway.

Then Maj. Clifford Reese brought in his Vs of B-24s from the other Long Ranger squadrons. Moments later, a new cascade of bombs, thousand pounders, fell on the long enemy airstrip. Nearly 40% of the explosives struck home, gouging more than two dozen holes in the runway. Some of the bombs which missed the strip also hit buildings or parked aircraft. All total, the Long Rangers dropped 73 tons of bombs.

When the raid ended, Burnham brought the planes up to 22,000 feet, circled in a wide arc, and then headed east. "All crew members, don oxygen masks. We'll be staying high for the ride home."

"Roger, Colonel," Maj. Cliff Reese said.

Soon, the B-24s were gone. Then Lieutenant Nakase droned over the smoking drome with his surviving Zero pilots. He looked down at the potholed runway and cursed because he could not bring in his planes here. "The enemy has badly damaged the runway and we cannot land aircraft. We will fly south to the emergency field at Galela."

"Yes, Honorable Nakase," Flight Leader Tori Hiromichi answered.

Meanwhile, Col. Tom Musgrave led his Liberators of the 5th Bomb Group toward Kendari, in the southern part of the Celebes. Although the Bomber Baron airmen had not seen enemy planes during the long flight from Noemfoor Island, the crews became tense as they crossed the southern length of the Molucca Sea. Kendari was a major airbase and the 5th Group airmen expected swarms of interceptors to greet them before they reached target. But within 100 miles of Kendari, dense clouds loomed in the west. The weather front was intense, with thick formations more than a mile deep and almost reaching the surface of the sea. Musgrave swore, obviously dismayed. Then, he got a call from bombardier Fred Bonds.

"I don't think we can hit the target, Colonel."

"It doesn't look like it, Lieutenant," the 5th Group commander answered.

"What are we going to do?"

"I don't know. We'll fly on a little further. Maybe the weather is better up ahead."

Lt. Bonds did not answer.

The men aboard the Bomber Baron Liberators stared into the massive clouds under them. They were flying at 14,000 feet and there was no way they could hit anything from this height through the thick overcast. Finally, Bonds called the group commander again.

"I think we'll have to abort, sir," the bombardier said.

"Goddam it," Musgrave cried. "After we came all

this distance, it would be a shame to turn back."

"We got no choice, Colonel," Bonds insisted.

The 5th Group commander sighed. "Okay." He then called his pilots. "Target is closed in solid. We couldn't do a thing through this overcast. We're going back."

The crews of the 5th Group felt a mixture of disappointment and relief. They had come so far, and all for nothing. But still, they would not face heavy AA fire and interceptors as did the 307th Group. The planes of the 5th also rose to 22,000 feet while airmen donned oxygen masks. Then, the Liberators turned east and droned back to Noemfoor Island.

Far to the northward, Maj. Vernon Ekstrand led his 23 Liberators of the 90th Bomb Group toward Tarakan, Borneo. As the Jolly Roger B-24s reached the harbor, Ekstrand expressed surprise. He had not met a single enemy interceptor and not a single burst of ack ack fire.

"Goddamn," the major told co-pilot Ed Cromwell, "we caught them with their pants down."

Cromwell looked at the harbor ahead where a dozen maru freighters and oilers were hastily weighing anchor to escape before the expected B-24 attack.

"They'll never get away, Major," Cromwell grinned at Ekstrand.

"No way," the 90th Group leader returned the co-pilot's grin.

Moments later, from 14,000 feet, the Jolly Rogers unleashed 30 tons of bombs which exploded over a wide area inside Tarakan Harbor. An array of explosions hit six of the Japanese vessels. Two oilers ignited before the ships blew apart. Two of the freighters caught solid hits that ripped the vessels open before the marus settled to the bottom of the bay. Two more ships caught devastating hits that smashed their superstructures. However, these vessels did not sink.

When the attack ended, Ekstrand veered his big bombers 180 degrees, also rose to 22,000 feet, and then headed back to New Guinea. He felt elated. The 90th had sunk or disabled a half dozen ships in Tarakan Harbor without damage to a single plane and without loss or injury to a single crewman.

Far to the south, the Liberators of the 43rd Bomb Group found the Japanese at Balikpapan equally off guard. At 1230 hours, the Ken's Men B-24s droned over the harbor at 14,000 feet and unleashed 42 tons of bombs on the anchored enemy vessels. The 43rd Bombardiers had especially concentrated on the tankers, and American bombs hit squarely three oilers as well as two freighters. The high level aerial attack sank three of the ships, while damaging the third oiler and the second freighter. As the B-24s veered away from Balikpapan, they left a mass of fire and smoke in the harbor.

By late afternoon, the four U.S. heavy bomber groups were well on their way back to New Guinea. Three of the units had done a good job, while the unfortunate Bomber Barons had been forced to abort. The ground crews of these groups counted their returning planes with elation. During the dark evening hours, all of the B-24s had returned safely to base. Dead and injured had been minimal and confined to the 307th Group, whose B-24s were the only planes to meet interceptors and heavy AA fire. The day's efforts had been astonishingly worthwhile, despite the long flights deep into the enemy's East Indies.

Similarly, the light and medium U.S. bomb groups had struck Japanese airfields at Babo, Amboina, and Bitjoli without losses, and without a single crew member killed or injured. They had unloaded 23 tons of bombs on Bitjoli, 18 tons on Amboina, and 15 tons on Babo.

Gen. St. Clair Streett expressed delight when he read the action reports from the bomb groups: heavy damage to ships in Tarakan and Balikpapan Harbors, heavy damage at the airfields at Manado, Bitjoli, Amboina, and Babo—all without loss of aircraft. Streett's only disappointment was the aborted mission to Kendari, but tomorrow was another day and the 13th Air Force commander would finish on the 27th what his bombers had not accomplished today.

However the Japanese had no intention of getting caught off guard twice in a row.

Chapter Four

The Japanese had found increasingly difficult the task of dealing with growing Allied air strength as the Americans advanced westward into their inner empire. The suspected U.S. invasion of the Philippines would require a major defense effort. Thus, Gen. Kyoji Tomingo, CinC of the Japanese 6th Base Air Force, frowned irritably when he learned that the Americans had made multiple raids on the East Indies bases with relative ease. If the Americans repeated such air attacks with impunity, the Japanese would have no more ships and no more airfields to thwart any American advance toward the Philippines. He scolded Admiral Fuchida who promised to act at once.

On the afternoon of 26 September, Fuchida flew at once to Kudat, Borneo, the headquarters of the 7th Air Division. He then ordered the commanders under his 4th Air Fleet command to report here at once for a conference. By early afternoon the next day, Fuchida held his meeting. In attendance was Capt. Maseo Matsumae, commander of the 7th Air Division, and his Sentai commanders, Lt. Satoshi Anabuki of the 381st, Lt. Masayuki Nakase of the 382nd, and the squadron leaders of the 383rd and 384th. Also here was Capt. Kameo Sonokawa, of the 23rd Air Flotilla, along with his navy Kokutai commanders, Cmdr. Joyotara Iwami of the 22nd, Lt. Kuniyoshi Tanaka of the 19th, Lt. Cmdr. Nobuo Fujita of the 20th, and Sonokawa's 23rd Air Flotilla aide.

"I am pleased that all of you answered my summons with such haste," Admiral Fuchida began. "You are to be congratulated for your promptness, but I cannot say the same thing for your shameful conduct against the recent enemy air attacks. The Americans no doubt took great delight in these assaults which they carried out with near impunity. Such negligence on your part may well encourage them to carry out similar air assaults with great enthusiasm. They could well neutralize our East Indies airfields and then clear a route to both the Balikpapan oil refineries and the Philippines themselves. I need not remind you," he wagged a finger, "that the 6th Base Air Force depends on the Balikpapan petroleum plants for sixty-five percent of its aviation fuel. So, you can understand that without these refineries the air force in the Philippines will be crippled."

The officers at the table merely listened soberly.

"These attacks yesterday were obviously pre-liminaries to a probable attack on the Balikpapan refineries. The enemy knows that the 6th Base Air Force has been building up its strength in the Philippines to offer strong resistance to any American invasion attempt," Fuchida gestured. "They also know that the Balikpapan refineries are vital if we hope to stop further enemy incursions into our inner empire."

"We are aware of that, Honorable Fuchida," Colonel Matsumae said. "I have taken steps to strengthen the 7th Air Division Sentais at Babo, Amboina, and Manado. And I will soon send the 381st Sentai to Balikpapan."

"The 381st Squadron must move to Balikpapan at once, even today or tomorrow," Fuchida said. "The Americans struck shipping in Balikpapan Harbor yesterday, and tomorrow it may be the refineries."

"I understand, Admiral," Matsumae said.

Fuchida merely grunted.

Matsumae was somewhat piqued. He did not like his 7th Army Air Division under the command of a navy admiral. During his many years as an army air commander, Matsumae had become convinced that Imperial Japanese Army air units had always shown more ability, adeptness, and aggressiveness than did navy air units. He considered the army pilots and their commanders quite superior to naval Kokutai units as evidenced by the recent navy air group debacle in the Marianas carrier battle this past June. Matsumae expressed disappointment when his division had passed from the authority of the 4th Air Army to the authority of a navy commander.

However, Matsumae had been a victim of a directive from Tokyo. Imperial Headquarters had decided on unified commands to meet further Allied threats to the East Indies and the Philippines. At the urgings of the Philippines Forces CinC, Gen. Tomoyuki Yamashi, Tokyo had appointed General Tominga to command an expanded 6th Base Air Force that included both army and navy air units, while they combined all army and navy air units in the East Indies under the unified command of the 4th Air Fleet. Thus, both the navy's 23rd Air Flotilla with headquarters at Kendari in the Celebes and the 7th Air Division with headquarters at Kudat, Borneo, had come under Admiral Fuchida.

Despite his distaste for a navy superior, Matsumae understood the need for unified commands and he had made the best of it.

Fuchida now looked harshly at Captain Sonokawa. "And where were the pilots of the 23rd Air Flotilla yesterday? Why did they not rise in record numbers at Bitjoli, Amboina, and Kendari to attack these American interlopers?"

"The Americans attacked these bases early in the morning with light bombers to thwart interception of their long range bombers," Sonokawa said. "However, I will take measures to make certain that such inaction does not happen again."

"Let us hope not," Fuchida said. He scanned a sheet of paper in front of him and then looked at Colonel Matsumae. "You have in your command four sentais, Colonel, and you have indicated that one of them will go to Balikpapan."

"Yes, Honorable Fuchida," Matsumae answered, referring to a sheet of his own. "As you suggested, I will ask Lieutenant Anabuki to complete his movement of the 381st Sentai to Manggar Field no later than tomorrow. I have already been informed that the honorable General Ichabangese has made arrangements to house the 381st airmen and to furnish troops to service this sentai. I was also told that Makassar Base Force troops are working to improve the air facilities at Balikpapan and to lengthen the runways so we can have heavy bombers stationed there should such deployment become necessary. I may also send some aircraft from the 383rd Sentai at Babo and the 384th Sentai at Amboina to Balikpapan. These bases have become quite untenable in recent weeks and I am inclined to leave as few aircraft there as possible, only enough so they can be easily hidden from American bombers."

Fuchida scowled. "Are you saying, Colonel, that your air squadrons are incapable of defending their own airfields?"

"I would remind the Honorable Fuchida that the enemy has countless bombers and fighters in Cape Sansapor and the Schouten Islands," Matsumae said. "When their bombers attack us at Amboina, they bring with them a hundred escorting fighter planes. We are simply overwhelmed. The same may be said of Babo on the Vogelkop Peninsula, where enemy bombers make almost daily attacks. We can barely keep the runway open and we have continually lost parked aircraft there." He leaned forward. "Is the 4th Air Fleet willing to send us two or three hundred fighters to protect Amboina and Babo?"

Fuchida did not answer.

"I have concluded," Matsumae continued, "that we should keep Babo and Amboina only with enough aircraft to make night time harassment raids against the enemy in the Schouten Islands."

Again, Fuchida did not answer. Instead, he looked again at Captain Sonokawa. "And when will the kokutai from your 23rd Air Flotilla come to Balikpapan?"

"Lt. Commander Fujita will bring his Mitsubishi (Zero) and Kawasaki (Tony) fighter aircraft of the 20th Kokutai to Samarinda Field in Balikpapan within a day or two. We will, of course, keep the entire 22nd Kokutai at Kendari. Commander Iwami has at his disposal fifty fighter aircraft and thirty light bombers which could also be used as interceptors against American bombers. We will also keep the 19th Kokutai with about fifty fighters at Bitjoli." He looked at the 19th Kokutai commander. "Lt. Commander Tanaka has assured me that his early warning crews will not again show the neglect they did today."

"I have disciplined the men who failed to report promptly the approach of the enemy bombers over Bitjoli," Tanaka said. "I have warned them that we will mete out severe punishment for any similar failures in the future."

"We can assure you, Admiral, that the 23rd Air Flotilla will be ready for any new American incursions," Sonokawa said. "The 19th Kokutai will be the first line of defense against enemy aircraft coming westward, and the 22nd Kokutai at the Kendari will be the second line of defense. The Americans can expect aggressive interception in both Djailalo Passage and over the Molucca Sea. And," Sonokawa gestured, "any surviving Yankee bombers will most assuredly meet more than they can handle in Lt. Commander Fujita's 20th Kokutai if the enemy crosses Makassar Strait to attack Balikpapan."

Fuchida nodded and then addressed Col. Matsumae again. "And what of your 7th Air Division? Manado was attacked yesterday by the enemy's heavy bombers and the pilots of your 382nd Sentai failed to shoot down a single Yankee aircraft. Meanwhile, the enemy did considerable damage to your airfield. This is hardly a way to deal favorably with the enemy."

Colonel Matsumae squirmed uneasily before he answered. "Unfortunately, many of the pilots are young and inexperienced. Lieutenant Nakase has assured me that he has lectured his pilots severely and he will not tolerate a repeat of yesterday's disgraceful performance."

"Let us hope not," the 4th Air Fleet commander said. He flipped through more sheets in front of him and spoke again. "I must now speak of the attacks on our vessels at Tarakan and Balikpapan. The enemy caused us terrible losses in both seaports where they sank or damaged at least a dozen marus." He shuttled his glance between Matsumae and Sonokawa, and he then scowled. "Not a single aircraft rose to meet these intruders, and not a single anti-aircraft gun challenged the Yankee bombers. Admiral Toyoda is utterly infuriated and who can blame him?"

Matsumae did not answer and Fuchida continued. "I must tell you that General Anami and General Yamashita are equally irate. The fuel and supplies aboard those marus were vital to our Philippine and East Indies military units. You had aircraft at Kudat, Colonel Matsumae. Why did they not intercept the enemy bombers which attacked our vessels in Tarakan?"

Col. Matsumae scowled, then leered at Captain Sonokawa. "I must state, Honorable Tominga, that in my opinion the fault lies with the 23rd Air Flotilla. They maintain air units at Bitjoli in the Halmaheras. Surely, these bombers which attacked the marus at Tarakan must have flown on a course directly north of Bitjoli. The navy squadron should have intercepted the Yankee bombers over the Celebes Sea."

"We were too busy dealing with an enemy attack on our airfield to engage these high flying bombers," Sonokawa said. "You have a sentai at Manado. These

60

pilots did not stop the Yankee bombers who attacked your own airfield and even your own commander admits his army pilots performed disgracefully." When Matsumae did not answer, Sonokawa grinned smugly. "Perhaps your airmen at Kudat were too frightened to attack the enemy at Tarakan after the army fighter pilots at Manado failed so badly against the Yankee bombers."

Matsumae's neck reddened and he gestured angrily at the 23rd Air Flotilla commander. "I would remind the Honorable Sonokawa that he suffered no air attack at his base in Kendari. Perhaps you can explain why navy aircraft from this field did not intercept the enemy air formation that flew almost directly over Kendari on the way to attack shipping in Balikpapan."

"The weather over Kendari was unfavorable," Sonokawa said, "and we were unaware that enemy aircraft were flying toward Balikpapan."

"At least our pilots at Manado attempted to stop these interlopers," Matsumae sneered, "While the pilots at Kendari did not even man their aircraft."

"Gentlemen, I have heard enough," Fuchida cried angrily. Then, he looked harshly at both men before he spoke in a low, calm voice. "I would think that both of you understood the dire problem we face with an enemy who grows stronger each day, who becomes more bold, and who encroaches ever deeper into our empire. General Yamashita and Admiral Toyoda have spared no effort in their cooperative endeavor to prepare defenses for the expected American invasion attempt of the Philippines. General Anami, Admiral Morita, and I have worked diligently to coordinate a mutual defense for the Indies, especially at Balikpapan. I have tried to make certain that all air units, army or navy, take measures to stop the enemy's air force. We have faced enough danger from the enemy. Must we also endure petty squabbles between army and navy air commanders who blame each other for yesterday's failure?"

Neither Col. Matsumae nor Captain Sonokawa answered.

"There was enough negligence to blame every airman in both the 7th Air Division and the 23rd Air Flotilla," Fuchida gestured angrily.

Matsumae lowered his head, obviously embarrassed. Captain Sonokawa merely turned his head to mitigate his own shame.

"By this time tomorrow both an army and navy air unit will be in Balikpapan to defend the vital petroleum refinery," Fuchida said. "Am I to assume that the army and navy airmen will direct their energies to bickering among themselves instead of fighting a common enemy? To blaming each other if all does not go as expected?" He looked at Nobuo Fujita of the 20th Navy Kokutai. "In a day or two you and your airmen will join the airmen of the army's 381st Sentai. Will you emulate your commander and degrade these army airmen?"

Lt. Cmdr. Fujita did not answer. He felt trapped between loyalty for his flotilla commander and his duty to obey the 4th Air Fleet CinC. Fuchida then turned to Satoshi Anabuki. "And you, Lieutenant, how will you and your pilots of the 381st Sentai greet the navy pilots when they arrive in Balikpapan? Will you show contempt for them? Will you express jealousy because you must share the airfields and barracks with them? Will you disparage them as your 7th Air Division commander disparages the 23rd Air Flotilla commander?"

Lieutenant Anabuki enjoyed an esteemed reputation, for the 381st Sentai commander was an experienced pilot who had been fighting since 1939 in China. He had been a mere P/O then and he had risen successively to W/O, F/O, and then to lieutenant in command of a sentai. He had thus far downed more than 70 enemy aircraft, including more than 20 American planes. He had earned the respect and admiration of his superiors because of his dedication, aggressiveness, and leadership qualities. Thus, he willingly spoke his mind, unafraid of superiors.

"Honorable Fuchida," Anabuki said, "I believe that both Captain Sonokawa and Colonel Matsumae are sorely grieved because of our failures yesterday. They seek an answer for the poor showing of their airmen, and in their distress they have unwittingly blamed each other. Yet the blame for the failures lies with the squadron commanders, both army and navy, who did not fulfill their obligations. The air division and air flotilla commanders can only prepare us and urge us to fight honorably and aggressively against our enemies. The fault lies with base commanders like myself who allowed ourselves to become lax. Yes," the lieutenant gestured emphatically, "myself, Lieutenant Nakase, Commander Iwami, Lt. Commander Tanaka, and the others. On our shoulders fell the duty to meet and stop the Yankee air formations, and we failed in this duty."

"Lieutenant, you show great courage in your willingness to assume the blame for yesterday's shortcomings," Fuchida said, "but the responsibility rests with the 7th Air Division and 23rd Air Flotilla commanders."

"Please, Admiral," Cmdr. Iwami suddenly spoke, "I totally share Lieutenant Anabuki's opinion. Our own neglect has simply distressed the air commanders. I do not believe that army and navy commanders are unwilling to cooperative with each other."

"I can assure you, Honorable Fuchida," Lt. Anabuki spoke again, "I will welcome Lt. Commander Fujita and his naval pilots to Balikpapan. I will do all that I can to make him comfortable at the Makassar Army Base Force. I will work closely with the 20th Kokutai commander to plan a unified air defense."

"Honorable Admiral," Lt. Cmdr. Fujita now spoke, "I wish to echo Lieutenant Anabuki's sentiments. I too will do whatever is necessary to cooperate fully with the army pilots of the 381st Sentai."

Fuchida nodded, grinned, and then addressed again Colonel Matsumae and Captain Sonokawa. "I would suggest to both of you that you follow the advice of your subordinates. Only with a mutual commitment can we hope to succeed against the Americans."

When neither Matsumae nor Sonokawa spoke, Fuchida continued. "I leave all of you with these final words: return to your units and charge your airmen so they will make a maximum effort. We can surely expect the enemy to attempt further attacks on our East Indies bases and on our Borneo harbors, and surely they will attempt to bomb the refineries at Balikpapan. You and your pilots must show an

64

ultimate determination in their interceptor duties, for only with aggressiveness can we hope to defeat the Americans. And finally, be certain that coast watchers and radar operators are ever alert to report enemy air formations as quickly as possible."

"We will follow these instructions adamantly, Honorable Fuchida," Col. Matsumae said.

Fuchida nodded, shuffled through his papers, and then spoke again. "I have been also assured that 9th Fleet submarines and destroyers will continually patrol the Makassar Strait, Molucca Sea, and Djailalo Passage to observe enemy air movements from the east. These navy vessels will report such sightings to the nearest air base at once, and I expect aircraft to intercept immediately." He paused and then sighed. "If there is no further business, this meeting is closed."

When the conference ended, Col. Matsumae spoke with his sentai leaders, while Capt. Sonokawa spoke with his airmen. The 7th Air Division would have 70 fighters of the 381st Sentai at Balikpapan, another 50 fighters and 20 bombers of the 382nd at Manado, and 50 fighters and 30 bombers at Kudat. He would split the remainder of his planes, about 20 fighters and 20 bombers of the 383rd and 384th Sentais between his battered bases of Amboina in Ceram Island and Babo on New Guinea. The 23rd Air Flotilla would have 50 fighters of the 20th Kokutai at Balikpapan, 50 fighters and 30 Val bombers of the 22nd Kokutai at Kendari, and 20 fighters and 20 bombers of the 19th at Bitjoli, Halmahera.

Meanwhile, by 0100 hours, 27 September, the 9th Fleet began its submarine and destroyer patrols in the sea lanes of the East Indies between New Guinea and

Borneo. Both the I-boats and tin cans carried radar for easy detection of American air formations.

On the morning of 27 September, American air commanders of FEAF's bomber groups once more briefed their crews: Maj. Vern Ekstrand of the 90th Group, Col. Jim Potty of the 43rd, Col. Tom Musgrave of the 5th, Col. Bob Burnham of the 307th, and the commanders of the U.S. medium and light bomb groups. They would go out again today to hit the Japanese bases at Babo, Amboina, Bitjoli, Manado, and Kendari. But at 0700 hours, all missions were scrubbed because of severe weather fronts that had closed on the East Indies, stretching all the way from Singapore into northern Australia and as far east as the Vogelkop Peninsula in New Guinea. Cloud depths were estimated at one to two miles, with a ceiling of less than 1,000 feet.

Thus, a respite came to the Japanese on this September day and they made the best of it. They worked feverishly to clear ships out of Balikpapan and Tarakan Harbors, to complete repairs on damaged runways, to load fighter planes for interceptor duties, and to transport AA gunners and fighter pilots to Balikpapan. 28 September dawned as badly as the day before with the heavy weather front still hanging over the East Indies. Thus American hopes to carry out more air attacks on the Japanese bases was again thwarted.

On the late afternoon of 28 September 1944, Col. John Murtha, the 13th Air Force operations officer, came into Streett's ADVON headquarters at Noemfoor. "Sir, we've got a new report from meteorologists. The weather is beginning to clear. They say we can probably fly out tomorrow. Shall we initiate the six-sixty missions?"

General Streett turned and peered from the open window of his quonset hut. He stared at the gray, low hanging clouds for a moment and then turned to his aide. "Scratch the six-sixty missions. Put FO 671 into effect."

Murtha's eyes widened. "You mean the refineries?"

"Yes."

"But sir, what about the raids on enemy airbases?"

"We can't wait any longer," Streett said. "We start the refinery raids now. Notify the 5th, 307th, and 90th Bomb Groups that the refinery mission is on for tomorrow."

The operations officer did not answer.

"They do have FO 671, don't they? They know what it's all about?"

"Yes sir."

"I want them off by 0200 hours. That gives them about ten hours to ready themselves."

"I'll notify the B-24 group commanders at once, sir." But, Murtha felt uneasy. The heavy bomber crews, without escorts and without knocking out those enemy Indies airbases, could suffer near disaster before they completed the 2360 mile round trip to Balikpapan.

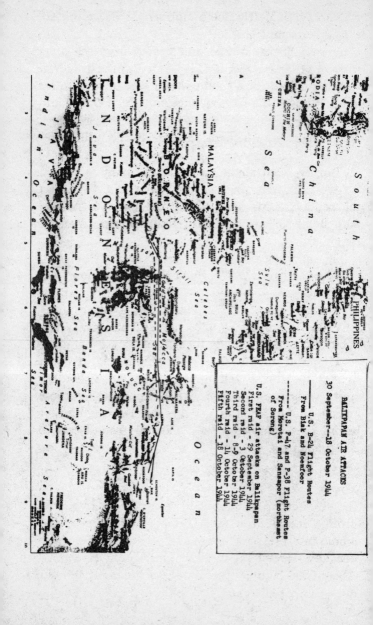

BALIKPAPAN AIR ATTACKS

30 September--18 October 1944

—— U.S. B-24 Flight Routes
From Biak and Noemfoor

—— U.S. P-47 and P-38 Flight Routes
From Morotai and Sansapor (northeast
of Sorong)

U.S. FEAF air attacks on Balikpapan
First raid - 29 September 1944
Second raid - 3 October 1944
Third raid - 8-9 October 1944
Fourth raid - 14 October 1944
Fifth raid - 18 October 1944

Chapter Five

Every American in the FEAF heavy bomb groups knew that sooner or later they'd be going to Balikpapan. Yet, when the order reached the B-24 groups at about 1700 hours on the evening of 28 September, a fear gripped the U.S. flyers who would be included on the mission. The combat crews learned that Balikpapan lay nearly 1200 miles away and the entire route ran through enemy territory. True, the 90th Bomb Group and 43rd Bomb Group had hit the Tarakan and Balikpapan Harbors only recently, and they had returned without loss. But, the Jolly Roger and Ken's Men crewmen had caught the Japanese by surprise, for the enemy apparently did not believe the Americans would come so soon to Borneo. The U.S. airmen were not likely to catch the enemy napping again. The U.S. airmen also recognized that the enemy had enjoyed two days of respite to prepare an aerial and AA defense all the way from New Guinea to Borneo.

FO 371 called for the 5th Bomb Group to strike first, followed by the 307th Group and then the 90th Group.

When group commanders received the FO order from General Streett's ADVON headquarters, they immediately selected crews and told them to sleep for the next several hours. The men would take off at about 0200 hours in the middle of the night. Evening

OD personnel would awaken them for briefing shortly after midnight.

By 0030 hours, in their respective squadron mess halls, the 26 ten man crews of the 5th Bomb Group ate a meal of hot bully beef, dehydrated potatoes, and canned green beans, with plenty of coffee. Cooks gave each man a box lunch meal of spam sandwiches and a thermos bottle of coffee to nourish them during the long round trip that would take 12 to 14 hours.

At 0045 hours the nearly 300 crewmen crammed into the double three poled tent for briefing. Bomber Baron aides started generators to furnish lighting and a microphone, and they readied wall maps and benches. Then Captain William Stewart cried "Tenshun" as Musgrave entered the tent. The airmen rose stiffly to their feet, while the operations officer tapped the mike on the podium to make certain the PA was working properly. The men watched Col. Tom Musgrave come to the podium where he gestured to the crews.

"At ease."

The crews relaxed and sat down before Musgrave nodded to the operations officer. "Captain, pass out maps to all pilots, navigators, and bombardiers."

"Yes sir," Stewart said. He then looked at the crowd of airmen. "Will all pilots, navigators, and bombardiers please raise your hands so our non-coms will know where to pass the maps." When several dozen hands went up, the captain waved to the sergeants and corporals. "Okay, pass out maps."

Musgrave waited until non-coms had passed out maps, but he fidgeted impatiently and looked at his watch. Take off time was at 0200 and he needed to brief his crews thoroughly. Finally, Capt. Stewart turned to the Bomber Baron commander. "Maps distributed, sir."

"Good." Then the colonel turned to a big map on the improvised wall behind him. "This is the target in case some of you still don't know who's going to Borneo. The Balikpapan refineries are on the east coast of the island. We expect to make a 2350 mile round trip and we'll probably be airborne for 12 to 14 hours. This will be one of our longest and most ambitious missions yet in the SWPA. These refineries at Balikpapan furnish at least half of the fuel and gasoline supply for the Japanese war machine in the western Pacific, particularly for their planes. In recent weeks, most of the enemy's opposition has been coming from their air force. So if we knock out the refineries, we can ground most of their planes."

The bomber crews listened.

"As you can see, we'll be following a near direct route from Noemfoor. We'll fly west and slightly north across the Djailalo Passage, cross the Halmaheras south of Ditjoli, then over the Molucca Sea, and then across the Celebes well south of Manado and north of Kendari. When we get halfway across Makassar Strait, we'll turn southwest into target—Balikpapan."

When Musgrave finished tracing the flight route, he nodded and his operations officer stepped close to the podium. Stewart then referred to a sheet in his hand before he spoke. "This is Field Order number 371 as you pilots, navigators, and bombardiers can see. You'll note that you'll be flying in a two section formation and your target will be the Pandansari Refinery. The first section will include six aircraft from the 31st and 23rd Squadrons, and the second section will include six aircraft from the 394th and 72nd Squadrons. Colonel Musgrave will lead the first section and Major Jim Pierce will lead the second section. Take off will be at about one minute intervals, the usual pattern for night missions. Once airborne, all aircraft will assume 130 degree turns for assembly into formation over Cape Manimbajo at 119 degrees."

"Squadron leaders will use colored flares to aid in assembly," Col. Musgrave spoke again.

"Red flares for the 31st, green for the 23rd, white for the 22nd, and yellow the for 394th," Capt. Stewart said. "Route speed will be at 160 MPH to conserve fuel, and altitude will be at about 8,000 feet."

"Will we all fly at the same altitude?" a pilot asked.

"No," Stewart said. "31st will fly at 8,500, 23rd at 8,000, 72nd at 9,500, and 394th at 9,000."

"When we near target," Musgrave said, "we should be on a 90 degree bearing, true, for the axis bomb run. All sections will be in bombing formation before we reach IP. Lead bombardiers from each squadrons will set range and deflections, and other bombardiers will sight for range only. Lieutenant Bonds on my lead A/C 595 will drop the pathfinder flare."

"Sir," Lt. Ken Guthiel asked, "will all planes from our group hit the Pandansari Refinery?"

"Not only us, Lieutenant, but a squadron behind us from the 307th Group will also hit the refinery," Musgrave answered. "This is the main plant of the Balikpapan complex and we want to make sure we knock it out."

"Yes sir," Guthiel answered.

"Now—the bombing run itself," Captain Stewart

gestured. "The run will be made after a 270 degree turn, as Colonel Musgrave pointed out." He then referred to a second wall map. "As you can see, here's the oil complex on Balikpapan Bay. The Pandansari edifice is right here at the north end of the complex. It's on a street one block beyond these four storage tanks, and one block before this walled in rectangular area, and just about on the shoreline of this small inland bay. This is a new, modern refinery that's essential for the distillation of aviation gasoline. According to intelligence reports, the plant refines about thirty million gallons of aviation gas and engine fuel annually. So you can understand how badly we can hurt the enemy if we destroy the plant."

"The first section should be over target at about 0940 hours, with the 31st Squadron bombing from 12,500 feet and the 23rd Squadron bombing from 12,000 feet," Col. Musgrave said. "Second section should reach IP about 1000 hours. The 394th will bomb at 13,000 feet and 72nd will bomb at 13,500 feet. As most of you know, all aircraft will carry ten 250 pound demo and incendiary bombs, only about forty percent of normal bomb load. But, since we'll be carrying 3,500 gallons of gasoline on this very long flight from Noemfoor, we can't carry a heavier bomb load."

"On the first two missions, your purpose is to fracture the oil complex and set fire to the installations," Stewart said, "and thus put them out of business temporarily. On subsequent missions, you'll be using heavier bombs to destroy the target area."

Musgrave now leaned over the podium and peered at his bomber crews before he once again gestured.

"Once we're beyond Cape Sansapor we'll maintain radio discipline. Only aircraft in distress have permission to break silence, and such distressed aircraft will use the 6280 tactical VHF channel to report its position in the event the plane must ditch in the sea. VHF communication on A Channel, 4475 Kcs, will be used for interplane contact."

"Call code for our group is Zorina, 1A to 1G for the 31st Squadron, 2A to 2G for the 23rd, 3A to 3G for the 72nd, and 4A through 4G for the 394th," the operations officer spoke again. "The 307th Group will be using the code Ranger and the 90th Group will be coded Bison."

"What about interceptors, sir?" Lt. Jim Russell asked.

"The Japanese could fly out of Bitjoli, Kendari, Manado, and maybe even from Borneo," Musgrave admitted. "But, we'll be passing over the Halmaheras and most of the Celebes in darkness, so they'd need to send night fighters after us, and they've never been very good at night interception. Of course, it'll be daylight before we clear the Celebes, and I don't know what we'll find over Balikpapan or what we might run into on the way back to Noemfoor. However, if you hold a tight formation, we'll have plenty of firepower and we might discourage interceptors."

"Yes sir," Russell said.

"How about rescue, sir?" Lt. Gutheil spoke again.

"If you'll refer to page three of the FO sheet, you'll see that FEAF has assigned one submarine and three Catalinas for rescue operations," Col. Musgrave said. "The submarine will be about five miles off the Borneo shoreline and their monitor is on VHF

Channel D, and their command is on radio frequency 4475. If you get hit hard and need to abandon ship, try to at least clear the coast for a few miles before you ditch. The code for submarine rescue is Blow Hard. Just give them your position and nothing else. Nothing! Understand?"

The crew members nodded.

"Once Blow Hard has acknowledged your position, stay put," Musgrave gestured. He looked at the sheet on the podium and then continued. "We'll also have two of the PBY flying boats in the area as far west as the middle of Makassar Strait. Catalina Daylight Eleven will orbit on station at 01 degrees south by 121 degrees east from 1000 to 1300 hours. Catalina Daylight Twelve will be on station at 01 degrees south by 127 degrees during the same hours. We'll have the third PBY off Sansapor, Daylight Thirteen. This plane will be on station from 1500 to 1730 hours. FEAF believe if you make it beyond Makassar Strait, you can probably make it to the Vogelkop Peninsula. By then, you should know whether or not you need to ditch, whether you can make the emergency landing strip at Sansapor, or if you can make it back to Noemfoor."

"If you'll look at the last page of the FO order," Captain Stewart said, "you'll see the code words for rescue status: Goodyear for survivors on life rafts, Yellow Jacket for survivors in the water with life jackets, and Davey Jones for survivors in the water without life jackets. Naturally, Blow Hard or Daylight will try to rescue Davy Jones survivors first, then Yellow Jackets, and then Goodyears."

75

"Please study the seven items for possible rescue," the colonel said. "It's vital that you follow each step. Be sure you tell Blow Hard or Daylight the nautical mile distance from rescue point, be sure you give a true bearing of your position, report the number of survivors, report the type of aircraft loss—in our case Mike for B-24. If you use your green markers, use the code word Evergreen, so potential rescuers can look for this dye color on the water's surface."

"We understand," Maj. James Pierce said.

However, the more Musgrave and Stewart talked about rescue, the more tense the airmen became. They had seldom heard so much detail on rescue at briefings and the combat crews feared the worst—many of them would go down from enemy AA and fighter interceptors. They remained glumly silent as Musgrave continued.

"I believe you should pass around the FO sheets while in flight so that every crew member can familiarize himself with the details, especially with the rescue formula."

"A good idea," Maj. James Pierce said.

"Any questions?" the 5th Bomb Group commander asked.

None.

"Okay, mount up," the Bomber Baron commander said. "Jeeps and personnel carriers are waiting outside."

An explosion of ad libs erupted among the men as they rose from their benches and funnelled out of the double operations tent with fellow crew members. Few of them relished the long mission to Balikpapan, but they steeled themselves for the 14 hour flight, and each man hoped he would be among those who returned to Noemfoor Island. When the loaded vehicles roared away, Capt. William Stewart and his staff snapped off lights in the operations tent and cut the generators. These men could go back to sleep in their tent quarters because they would not see their planes and crews again until sometime in the afternoon.

Less than a mile away, in a similar canvas operations tent, Col. Bob Burnham held a similar briefing with 24 crews of his 307th Bomb Group. Like the men of the 5th, these Long Rangers also felt uneasy. They too had eaten a midnight meal at their squadron mess halls, and they too received box lunches to nourish them on the expected 12 to 14 hour flight. The 307th's B-24s would take off at the Kornasoren strip right behind the Liberators of the 5th Group. Burnham also explained the flight route from Noemfoor to Balikpapan, the call code for each squadron aircraft, and the formulae for rescue in case any aircraft ditched.

"We have no idea what kind of interception we might get over Balikpapan or how much ack ack fire we might encounter," Col. Burnham said. "The 43rd didn't meet a single Japanese plane or one burst of flak on their shipping mission a few days ago, but they obviously caught the Japs off guard. The enemy never expected our bombers to fly to Balikpapan, apparently. We can't expect to catch them asleep again, so we'll need to be ready for anything. All I can suggest is that you stay in tight formation, so you've got plenty of fire power. That usually discourages Japanese interceptor pilots."

"Are we going after the main refinery?" Lt. Ron Covington asked.

"Only our 372nd Squadron," Burnham said. "The 5th Group will precede us and all of their aircraft will hit the Pandansari plant, with our 372nd also hitting this plant. Major Reese's 370th Squadron will hit the paraffin plant and the 373rd will hit the storage tanks, pipelines, or anything else in the complex."

"I see," Lt. Covington said.

"I cannot overemphasize the need to maintain tight formation," Burnham said again.

"What's the weather picture, Colonel?" Major Cliff Reese asked.

"Broken clouds for most of the way according to the latest meteorology reports."

"What if the target's closed in?"

"Then we bomb the best we can with H2X radar," the Long Ranger commander said. "We sure as hell won't fly all that way and then abort."

"Yes sir."

Burnham referred to a large map of the Balikpapan complex on a wall board behind him. "You can see the complex on this chart that was made from recent aerial photographs. We'll be coming into target at a 270 degree course. Here's the Pandansari aviation fuel refinery. The aircraft of the 372nd will bomb the plant along with the 5th Group at 14,000 feet. Major Reese's 370th Squadron will hit the paraffin-lube oil plant just south of the Pandansari plant from 14,500 feet. The 373rd will hit the complex of fuel storage tanks, pipelines, and warehouses just south of the Pandansari complex. Any of you have questions?"

"What about the 90th Group?" Reese asked.

"I believe they've drawn the Edeleanu sulfuric acid plant to the east," the colonel said. "Are there any more questions?"

Before anyone spoke, they heard the drone of planes in the night sky. The aircraft were B-24s from the 90th Group which had flown to Noemfoor from Biak Island. The Jolly Rogers would stage from Noemfoor for their mission to Balikpapan, for even the short 100 mile flight from Biak offered the 90th Group at least a little extra range for the long flight to Borneo. Then the putting sound of jeeps and growling of personnel carriers radiated from the parking area outside of the operations tent. The vehicles waited to carry the Long Rangers to their big Liberators on Kornasoren Field. Burnham again scanned his crews and when no one spoke, the colonel nodded.

"Okay, let's mount up."

As did the men of the 5th Group, these 307th Group airmen also chattered with each other as they left the tent and walked to waiting vehicles.

By the time the combat crews of the 5th and 307th reached their aircraft, the planes of the 90th had alighted on the Kornasoren Field and pulled off into revetment areas where they waited to follow the 13th Air Force groups off the air strip. Maj. Vernon Ekstrand would lead the 23 Liberators of the 90th Group, six planes from three Jolly Roger squadrons, and five from the fourth squadron.

Ekstrand sat in his lead A/C 367 and peered from the cockpit into the darkness to watch the planes of the other heavy bomb groups rock over the taxiways toward the runway with lights glaring. They resembled huge, carnivorous black widows that were stalking prey. Eckstrand could also see the scintillating lights coming from the control tower at the far end of the strip, a mixture of whites, reds, and yellows. The tower reminded him of a Christmas tree lit up during the holiday season. Also about the field, vehicles of every description scooted over the flats in a dozen directions, carrying combat airmen, crew chiefs, mechanics, and dispersal personnel who would aid in take offs.

At 0200 hours Musgrave led his lead B-24 of the 5th Group to the head of the runway. As the green light blinked from the control tower, a mile away, he released the brakes and sped down the runway with the plane's landing lights showing the way. In the nose gun position, Sgt. Harold Trout watched apprehensively. As long as he could see the runway ahead, he felt safe, and he hoped the plane would leave the ground before the B-24 reached the end of the strip. For a full half minute that seemed like an hour, Trout kept his eyes glued to the lighted patch of runway. Then, his tenseness eased when the big bomber rose upward into the night sky.

Trout had reason to worry. The B-24 carried more than $1\frac{1}{3}$ of its normal fuel load and even this strong, heavy bomber might have difficulty in getting off the ground. Soon, the gunner saw only a clear sky ahead of him and, when the colonel shut off the landing lights, the twinkling stars became much more pronounced to the young gunner.

In the ball turret, Sgt. Marv Anderson peered down at the array of lights from the hordes of planes still waiting to take off and from the many vehicles moving about the field. From the tail section, Sgt. Jim Shaw also peered down at the array of moving jeeps, trucks, and aircraft.

Behind Musgrave, a half minute later, Lt. Jim Russell sped down the dark runway with landing lights blazing. His crew also felt uneasy as the heavily laden B-24 rolled down the strip, picking up speed with each yard. Gunners Joe Tribble and Chuck Smith and Hal Philipps, in the turret and waist positions respectively, felt the struggling B-24 strain to leave the ground. They stiffened until Russell finally brought the big bomber upward. The three gunners peered into the darkness beyond their positions to await other aircraft from the 5th Group which would jell into formation with their own plane.

The third Bomber Baron plane, that of Lt. Ken Guthiel, now roared down the long Kornasoren runway and here too, Sgt. Les Barker in the waist and Sgt. Chuck Lee in the top turret waited stiffly until *Blackjack* rose off the runway. Like other crew members, these two gunners detested the heavy fuel load, and they also worried about taking off until the plane finally rose skyward.

Then, with each passing minute, other planes from the 5th Group also roared down the runway and took off. Soon the 24 planes had risen safely skyward into the dark, moonless night.

Next came the 24 B-24s of the 307th which also took off at one minute intervals. By 0240 hours, all of the Long Ranger planes were airborne without mishap. The two groups had left the field sooner than expected and now the 23 planes from the 90th Group lumbered to the head of the runway. Soon, the green light blinked again from the control tower and one by one the Jolly Roger B-24s roared down the airstrip and soared skyward.

When the Noemfoor Island airfield had been stripped of its horde of planes, ground crews below listened to the whining aircraft in the darkness above. They could not see the B-24s clearly, but they guessed that the Liberators were turning and rising to meld into formation somewhere over Cape Manimbajo. When the sound of planes diminished to the northwest, the ground personnel ambled to their vehicles. In near silence, they boarded jeeps and trucks for the ride back to camp. None of them expected to see every plane return this afternoon as the B-24s had returned from the 26 September mission.

The ground crews would return to their messhalls, drink coffee, conjecture on what might happen, and then flop on cots in their tents to sleep. At least 12 hours would pass before they saw their planes and combat crews again.

By 0330 hours, 29 September, the Kornasoren airfield had become dark and deserted. All lights were out in the control tower, vehicles had left the airfield, and a serene quiet had settled on the coral flats of Noemfoor Island.

Meanwhile, the 71 FEAF Liberators had merged into formation over Cape Manimbaja and now droned westward at 8,000 feet. Aboard the 5th Group aircraft, the crews stared from their windows into the dark night to scan the twinkling stars above or the black shapes of fellow B-24s that hung in the sky like suspended dragon flies. Col. Tom Musgrave sat quietly in the lead A/C 595 and stared at the emptiness ahead. In the nose, Sgt. Harold Trout peered up at the starry sky, while gunner Marv Anderson from his belly turret looked down at the black sea below. Bombardier Fred Bonds squinted into the emptiness ahead of them and gunner Jim Shaw, in the tail, studied the B-24 diamonds behind him.

Aboard A/C 572, pilot Jim Russell shuttled his glance between the colonel's plane and the emptiness ahead. In the top turret, gunner Joe Tribble yawned, already tired before the long flight had even begun. In the waist position, Sergeants Hal Phillips and Charlie Smith drank coffee from their thermos jugs. On A/C 607, Lt. Ken Guthiel checked his instruments, while gunner Chuck Lee in the turret of *Blackjack* checked his guns, and waist gunner Wes Barker checked an ammo belt.

Aboard the lead A/C 951 of the 307th Group, Col. Bob Burnham also stared into the black night beyond the cockpit, while co-pilot Joe Rodrick checked the oil pressure gauge. In the nose bombardier Wes Brown checked the Norden sight, while Sgt. Ed Anderson swung his .50 caliber guns to make sure they were loose. In the waist, Sgt. Sam Leffort slumped on the floor to get a little sleep. Aboard A/C 589, Lt. Ron Covington checked his instrument panel, while gunner Ralph O'Brien toyed with his 50 caliber machine guns to occupy himself.

Behind the 5th and 307th Groups, in the lead Liberator of the 90th Group, Maj. Vern Ekstrand checked his map with his co-pilot, Lt. Ed Cromwell, to make sure they had pinpointed their target, the Edeleanu plant that produced the sulphuric acid that was so vital for the solvent treatment of aviation gasoline. In the lower nose section bombardier Will Abeil checked his map with a pen light. He would direct the bomb run on the Edeleanu plant. Meanwhile, waist gunners Frank Gutierre and Al Tulley stared from their respective left and right windows at the dark shapes of fellow B-24s droning westward with them. They could talk later, for they'd have plenty of time on this 12 to 14 hour flight.

In *Mann's Morons,* Pilot Frank Mann stared straight ahead as did his co-pilot, Lt. Al Behm. They had already checked their maps and instruments so they could do nothing more than sit and wait.

In the Jolly Rogers lead 319th Squadron aircraft, *Phyllis J. of Worcester,* Maj. Charles Briggs and co-pilot Hank Pennington had also checked their maps and instruments. Further, Briggs had already checked twice with his crews to make certain all stations were in proper order. In the fuselage, Navigator Tom Glassman plotted his course on a map table, although he really had no need to do so since his B-24 merely followed the other Liberators in the 71 plane formation. In the top turret, Sgt. Steve Novak stared into the blackness around him and the ebon shapes of fellow Liberators that dangled in the sky like distorted monsters which had emerged from an alien planet. In the tail fellow gunner Henry Clay looked at the big bombers of the 321st Squadron that brought up the rear of this mile long string of FEAF B-24s.

Then at 0400 hours, a call came from Col. Tom Musgrave, the mission commander. "This is Zorina leader to all Zorina, Ranger, and Bison aircraft. We are now approaching check point one (Halmaheras). All gunners stay alert. This will be the last communication; we maintain radio discipline the rest of the way."

Every gunner aboard every B-24 reacted swiftly and manned his guns. Despite the darkness, enemy interceptors could loom out of the night from the Japanese base at Bitjoli or other bases in the Halmaheras; or they might come from the enemy base at Amboina on Ceram Island.

Chapter Six

In Djailalo Passage, the destroyer *Samidare* had been patrolling the waters in a north-south shuffle all day on 28 September and into the night and next day and night. Lookouts and radar men had been alert for many hours. But, ironically, the destroyer had been on its most southerly point when the Liberators cleared Djailalo Passage and reached the Halmahera coastline. Thus the Japanese sailors had missed the American B-24 formation. On Halmahera itself, however, coast watchers heard the drone of aircraft in the skies and they immediately reported the planes to the 19th Kokutai headquarters at Bitjoli. As soon as the night OD received the message, he roused Lt. Cmdr. Kuniyoshi Tanaka out of bed. However, the Kokutai leader scowled and then cursed.

"Bakkyra! They have chosen to fly during the dark hours. Our pilots are all asleep except for a three aircraft patrol, and our fighters sit coldly on the airfield. We cannot possibly attack these aircraft before the enemy formation has passed us by. Anyway, we are not equipped for night time interception."

"No, Honorable Commander."

"You will notify the OD's at Kendari and Manado at once," Tanaka gestured, "and tell them to expect enemy aircraft over Celebes Island in about two hours. It will then be almost daylight and perhaps they can intercept the Americans."

"Where would these Yankee bombers be going at such an hour?" the OD asked.

"I would guess they are flying to Balikpapan," Tanaka said, "no doubt to attack the refineries sometime in the morning. Call Manado and Kendari," he said again. "You should also notify the Makassar Base Force headquarters in Balikpapan."

"Yes, Commander," the OD said.

The first hint of daylight had emerged in the east by the time the B-24 formation reached the Celebes, but ahead lay thick cumulus clouds. Musgrave called his air commanders and ordered them to 14,000 feet. As the 5th Group commander looked at the dense cover, he felt frustrated. He feared this heavy cover might be even worse over Balikpapan and the target would be completely closed in. However, Musgrave was determined to hit the refineries, even if he had to bomb by H2X radar.

Yet the cloud cover over the Celebes was a blessing for the Americans. At Manado, Lt. Masayuki Nakase had risen skyward with 30 fighter planes and headed southward to meet the B-24s, while from Kendari, Cmdr. Joyatoro Iwami took off with 24 Oscars and Tonys to meet the FEAF bombers. However, the dense clouds thwarted any interception. B-24 radio men observed the approaching planes on their radar screens and Col. Tom Musgrave took his 71 Liberators down to 8,000 feet, deep inside the heavy cloud banks. He then flew westward by radar. So neither the Japanese 382nd Sentai from Manado, nor the 22nd Kokutai from Kendari could find the American aircraft.

"They hide in the cloud banks, Honorable Nakase,"

Flight Leader Tori Hiromichi called his 382nd commander.

"True," Nakase answered his F/O. "They have acted wisely. We cannot engage them deep inside the overcast, for we may run into each other. No, we can only notify the Makassar Base Force headquarters in Balikpapan to expect these enemy bombers sometime at mid-morning."

"Yes, Lieutenant," Hiromichi said.

Similarly, Lt. Susumu Ishihara called Joyotara Iwami, commander of the 22nd Kokutai out of Kendari. "We have been frustrated again, Honorable Commander," the flight leader said. "The enemy has hidden in the clouds and I believe it would be perilous to attempt any engagement in these clouds."

"Admiral Fuchida will express his wrath once more, if we do not intercept," Commander Iwami said. "But I must agree with you. There is no possibility of attacking the American bombers in this heavy overcast without endangering ourselves. We will notify the Makassar headquarters to expect the Yankee formation in about three or four hours. The enemy aircraft must have heavy fuel loads for their long flight from New Guinea, and they cannot be flying with much speed. It will take them a few hours to cross the Celebes and Makassar Strait."

Thus the Americans successfully avoided interceptors from both the Halmaheras and Celebes air bases. Soon, the B-24s cleared the Celebes and droned over Makassar Strait, the last stretch to Borneo's east coast.

At Balikpapan, word of the approaching bombers reached the base headquarters at about 0600 hours. The OD officer quickly roused Gen. Shosho Ichabangese out of bed and the base commander dressed hurriedly in whatever clothes he found handy. The general scowled in irritation for he found quite distasteful this intrusion into his quiet, comfortable life. The Makassar Base Force commander could not enjoy his usual leisurely and hearty breakfast this morning for he needed to hurry into the radio room where an aide would serve him a simple cup of tea.

Ichabangese had experienced his first taste of war a few days ago when the B-24s of the 43rd Bomb Group had struck Balikpapan Harbor, sinking three vessels and damaging others. He had watched the bombardment in horror; not because of the damage to shipping, but because the air attack had abruptly changed his life in Balikpapan from one of contented ease to one of sober wartime reality. Worse, the friendly citizens of Balikpapan had grown uneasy. They had accepted the raid on the refineries about a year ago by the U.S. 380th Bomb Group as a mere symbolic raid, but would the Americans now bomb their beautiful city in Borneo on a regular basis?

General Ichabangese had tried to assure the Indonesians that the American attack on the harbor shipping was another isolated bombing raid, but the civilians were no longer convinced. They had seen the military activity in and around Manggar Field: the arrival of anti-aircraft guns and their crews, the advanced echelon of the 20th Combat Kokutai, the appearance of the 381st Combat Sentai with its planes and crews, and the tons of military supplies unloaded on the docks. For the first time since Japan overran the East Indies, the Indonesians now doubted that

Japan could protect them against the return of the Dutch colonialists. Such skepticism did not please Ichabangese.

"Reports from the Celebes say that enemy bombers are expected by mid-morning," The OD told the general.

"I see," Ichabangese scowled.

"Unfortunately, Honorable General, Lt. Nobuo Fujita has not yet arrived in Balikpapan with the fighter planes of the 20th Kokutai. Only the advanced echelon is here."

"What of the anti-aircraft battalion?"

"Major Magari has thus far only established six gun positions, and he is not expected to ready the other guns of his 246th Battalion for another two or three days. So, we have only Lieutenant Anabuki's 381st Sentai aircraft and about a dozen anti-aircraft guns to meet these bombers."

"Still," the general said, "you will notify Major Magari at once to alert whatever gun crews are prepared so they can attack the enemy aircraft. You will also notify Lieutenant Anabuki to intercept these American bombers. Perhaps the 381st Sentai can destroy these enemy aircraft or drive them off before they reach Balikpapan. How many bombers are in the enemy formation?"

"We do not know, but at least fifty. However, the enemy does not have fighter escorts with them. Balikpapan is too far from the enemy's base in New Guinea and well out of range of American fighter planes."

"It is my understanding that Lieutenant Anabuki has seventy fighters," the general said. "Without escorts the Americans will be no match for the 381st Sentai. I believe that Anabuki and his pilots can easily thwart a successful bombing attack."

The Makassar Base commander, who had never seen combat, naively believed that the heavily armed B-24s were easy pickings for Japanese fighter planes. The general was grossly ignorant of the Liberator's tough strength, the dedication of the well trained American bomber crews, and the sharp shooting ability of the B-24 gunners.

"It appears the Americans were unwise to send this many bombers so far without escorts," Ichabangese continued. "They surprised us three days ago, but they were foolish to believe they could do so again. Yes," he nodded, almost to himself, "our fighters should easily destroy these unescorted bombers, and local citizens will see that Japan still dominates the East Indies." Then he gestured sharply. "Call Lieutenant Anabuki and Major Magari at once," he said again. "You will also call the supervisor of the refineries and inform him that enemy bombers intend to attack the complex today. He must take all necessary precautions."

"Yes, Honorable General."

The Makassar Base Force commander left the radio room and hurried to his quarters, away from the reminder of war. Ichabangese then washed, dressed comfortably, and ambled to his luxurious dining room for a good breakfast. He had done his duty as far as he was concerned. If the Americans hurt the refinery, he could blame Anabuki and Magari for their failure to stop the intruders.

Lt. Satoshi Anabuki did not hesitate when, at 0700

hours, he received word from Makassar Base head-quarters that a formation of at least 60 heavy American bombers were on the way to Balikpapan to bomb the refineries. Anabuki quickly awoke his ground crews and ordered them to load and fuel all planes for interception. The 381st commander then ate a quick breakfast and called his fighter leaders into a briefing. He referred to a map on the wall behind him as he spoke.

"We can expect the enemy to approach the refineries from the west. I suspect they will circle over the mountains and come over Balikpapan Bay. Broken clouds lie overhead at the moment, but we cannot be sure the skies will be clear or overcast in the next three hours. We must be airborne to meet these bombers. We do know that the enemy planes have been identified as B-24s which usually bombard from 13,000 to 15,000 feet. So, we will maintain our station at 16,000 feet."

"How many Yankee bombers are there?" F/O Yashiko Kuroe asked.

"At least fifty, but the bombers do not have escorts."

Kuroe frowned; "Still, the B-24s carry massive arms, perhaps a dozen guns on each aircraft. They are huge, heavy, and strong; very difficult to shoot down."

Kuroe had been stationed in Truk during the B-24 raids last March on this Japanese stronghold, and he recalled vividly the six B-24 attacks. He had been among the few army pilots at Truk who had intercepted these American Liberators and his air unit had only shot down three B-24s while the Liberators' gunners had scored heavily against the Truk interceptors.

"Can seventy fighters deal with so many B-24s?" Kuroe asked Anabuki.

"We must do our best," the 381st commander answered, "We will destroy or damage as many of them as we can. If we show skill and aggressiveness and if we harass them continually, we can at least disrupt the aim of their bombardiers and perhaps they will miss the refineries altogether. Unfortunately, the navy aircraft have not yet arrived, and not all of the anti-aircraft guns are in readiness." He paused and then continued. "We will attack the Yankee bombers in single dives. Please be certain that each pilot of every flight is in a position to continue an attack immediately behind the aircraft in front of him. I cannot tell you the best angle of attack, for the B-24 has firepower from every direction. The flight leaders will need to use their own judgment."

"Yes, Honorable Anabuki," F/O Kuroe said.

Meanwhile, Maj. Toshio Magari called his anti-aircraft platoon leaders together and expressed dismay that only 12 of his 30 guns were ready for use. "I am discouraged because our guns and shells did not arrive earlier, for we cannot attack these intruders as heavily as I would have liked. Still, we must do our best." He looked at a sheet in his hand. "We have six guns on the coast, three to the northeast of the refineries, and three guns about the city itself. I believe the enemy will circle the hills and then fly in from the west to attempt their bombardment. It becomes incumbent upon the anti-aircraft gun crews on the coast, therefore, to carry out the major attack."

"Yes, Major," a platoon leader answered.

"We must assail the enemy aircraft as soon as they are within range. Our radar equipment is now established and you will have ample warning of the enemy's approach. I can only tell you to make certain that all crews are in all gun pits and that they have plenty of ammunition. It is my understanding that at least fifty bombers are on the way. So, you will have a quite busy morning."

"Can we expect these heavy enemy bombers to conduct their bombardment from the usual thirteen to fifteen thousand feet?"

"Yes," the major nodded, "so your gun crews should set their anti aircraft bursts for this altitude." Then Magari sighed. "Let us hope we can shoot down or seriously damage enough of these interlopers to severely disrupt any bombing accuracy on the refineries."

Both Lieutenant Anabuki and Major Magari prepared their pilots and AA gunners to meet the American air formation.

By 0920 hours, two of the Liberators had turned back with mechanical trouble, but the other 69 B-24s continued across Makassar Strait. In the bright morning, Musgrave yawned and he then peered at the thin, broken clouds ahead. The weather had cleared considerably and the 5th Bomb Group colonel hoped that perhaps they would see plenty of open sky to bomb visually. And soon, he saw the ridge of mountains that ringed Balikpapan and the area about the city. He then broke radio silence and called his squadron leaders, because Musgrave was certain the Japanese had detected the B-24s by now.

94

"We're climbing to 13,000 feet; then we'll make a 180 degree turn and come in over Balikpapan Bay for the bomb run. All Zorina aircraft will bomb the Pandansari Refinery as will Ranger aircraft 1A to 1F. The remainder of Ranger aircraft will attack the paraffin-lube plant. Bison aircraft will attack Edeleanu plant, east of the Pandansari refinery. Remember, maintain tight formation. We can certainly expect interceptors."

Musgrave had barely finished talking over this VHF inter-plane A Channel when Sgt. Harold Trout in the nose gun position cried into the intercom: "Bandits! Bandits at twelve o'clock!"

"Okay," Musgrave said. "Stay alert!"

Then at 0925, the lead B-24 squadron of the 5th Group got jumped by 30 planes: ten Zeros, ten Tonys, and ten Oscars under F/O Yasihiko Kuroe. The Japanese flight leader was especially anxious to knock down Musgrave's lead plane for he rightly guessed that the bombardier aboard this B-24 would set the bombing run. American gunners studied the enemy planes, most of them painted black with either white or red bands around their fuselages. The Japanese planes roared into the American bombers from nine and three o'clock, with most of the 381st fighter pilots loosening an array of 20mm and 7.7 fire at 400 yards. The attacks chopped holes in several of the 5th Group planes, but failed to down any.

Musgrave's lead aircraft, a prime target, caught hits in the plexiglass on the nose turret, in the tail turret, and in the pilot's window. One 20mm shell ripped along the starboard side of the fuselage, while another Japanese shell cut three 10 to 12 inch holes in the wing. But, miraculously, no one was hurt on the colonel's plane, while gunners on Musgrave's B-24 responded with heavy .50 caliber machine gun fire of their own. They scored with astonishing accuracy.

Nose gunner Harold Trout caught an Oscar as the plane roared downward on the Liberator from two o'clock. The sergeant fired 125 rounds at the enemy and the Oscar lost its tail. The plane dropped like a dead bird and plopped into Balikpapan Bay. Sgt. Marv Anderson, from his ball turret, caught a Zero that came toward the B-24 from 11 o'clock. Anderson fired 80 rounds into the enemy plane and hewed away part of the wing. The Zero turned over and then tried to straighten, but in vain. The plane crashed into the sea. Sgt. Jim Shaw, squinting through his shattered plexiglass, watched a Zero come in from seven o'clock. He raked the plane with machine gun fire and set the engine aflame. As the Zero dove away, Shaw sent more fire into the aircraft. The Japanese plane smoked badly, did a loop, and arced downward in a heavy trail of smoke before the plane crashed into some trees.

Other B-24s also caught serious hits. A/C 252 got a 3 inch hole in the left wing and a 1 inch hole in the bomb bay. Another Liberator sustained a punctured fuselage. A fourth 5th Group B-24 had its No. 3 engine oil line shattered and the pilot feathered the prop to avoid further damage.

Despite the Japanese interception, the 5th Group Liberators made their wide 180 degree turn and droned over Balikpapan Bay to make their bomb run. But now the Americans met heavy AA fire, with endless puffs of black smoke bursting about the U.S.

planes. Lt. Jim Russell's plane caught flak hits that damaged its left rudder, while a second Bomber Baron B-24 got hits in the right wing panel, engine nacelle, and armor plating below the bombsite. Ken Gutheil's B-24 from the 394th Squadron had its hydraulic system shot away from a flak burst, while another B-24 caught flak in the No. 1 and No. 4 stations of the fuselage.

However, gunners continued to score against the Japanese interceptors. Aboard Lieutenant Russell's plane, turret gunner Joe Tribble and waist gunners Charlie Smith and Hal Phillips ganged up on one Oscar and knocked the Japanese plane apart with .50 caliber fire. On Lt. Ken Gutheil's plane, waist gunner Wes Barker set a Zero afire, and as the plane wobbled away turret gunner Chuck Lee finished off the Japanese interceptor with a second heavy burst of machine gun fire.

Meanwhile, the 5th Group continued toward target. In the lead plane, despite damage, Bombardier Fred Bonds ignored the array of interceptors that still sent chattering fire, and he ignored the whooshing 20mm shells that laced the bomber formation. Bonds also disregarded the heavy bursts of flak that now exploded all about him. With steel nerves, Bonds carefully sighted the target through his Norden sight until he pinpointed the Pandansari Refinery, 13,000 feet below. Finally, he was over IP and he unleashed his pathfinder flare. Then he cried into his radio.

"Bomb away!"

Moments later, ten 250 pound bombs, demolition as well as incendiary, fell out of the belly of Musgrave's B-24 and exploded in and about the refinery plant. About half of the bombs struck home to start fires, and others near missed the big building. Other 250 pounders fell from other B-24s in the 5th Bomb Group formation. In fact, for 20 minutes, beginning at 0940 hours, 250 pounders dropped from bomb bays of the Bomber Baron Liberators.

All total, the 5th Group unloaded 180x250 bombs over the target, with about 60 of them striking home. One string of bombs walked across a group of fractionating towers, while another cluster of bombs exploded along the eastern side of the same area. A staccato of concussions erupted large fires that sent cherry colored flames rising upwards and billowing smoke spiralling some 6,000 feet into the air. Some of the 5th Group bombs landed southwest of the target and into Balikpapan Bay. Ironically, two bombs made direct hits on a Sugar Baker, sinking the small supply ship that was anchored at Pier 27.

Behind the 5th, the Long Rangers of the 307th also got jumped by Zeros and Oscars, some 25 of them under Lieutenant Anabuki. However, in their haste to hit the B-24s, the Japanese attacked with little coordination. They came from around the clock, but mostly with level front attacks and high lateral attacks. From above, some of the Oscars also dropped phosphorous bombs on the 372nd Squadron formation, but none of the bombs hit any American planes. Meanwhile, Gunner Joe Black aboard Lt. Ron Covington's plane riddled an Oscar that exploded within 500 feet of the B-24 before the fragments fell out of the sky. On Lt. Don Forke's plane, Gunner Ralph O'Brien got an Oscar that exploded in mid air and then cascaded downward in a fiery ball.

In turn, the attacking Japanese pilots had only caused moderate damage. One 307th Group Liberator had its pilot station and hydraulic system damaged from a 20mm shell burst and a second 372nd Squadron aircraft suffered a 20mm hit in the No. 2 station on the left side of the plane, killing the radio man-gunner and injuring the second waist gunner.

The Long Rangers came over target on schedule. In Col. Bob Burnham's lead plane, bombardier Wes Brown peered calmly through his Norden bomb sight, despite zooming enemy planes and bursting black puffs of AA all about the bomber. Because of heavy smoke rising from the Pandansari plant the bombardier could not see the target clearly. But he bombed by H2X radar and the seven planes of the 372nd dropped 20 250 pounders that erupted more explosions, fire and smoke.

Behind the 372nd Squadron Clifford Reese led the remaining 16 planes from the 307th Group. Only five of the planes, however, could find their targets because of cloud cover and they dropped 50 bombs on the paraffin-lube oil plant. About half of the bombs struck target, while others fell 100 to 500 yards off the mark. The other Long Ranger B-24s dropped their 250 pounders on targets of opportunity, mostly barracks, storage tanks, pipe lines, and power lines. Now explosions erupted more fire and smoke.

By the time the B-24s of the 90th Group came over target, the entire area had been well obscured by smoke. Also, the cloud cover had worsened to further hide their target—the Edeleanu sulfuric acid plant. Maj. Vern Ekstrand, leading the Jolly Rogers, scowled in frustration. His bombardiers had no idea where to find the plant. He called his pilots.

"We'll need to hit targets of opportunity. That petroleum complex is certainly big enough to find plenty to hit down there."

"Okay, Vern," Maj. Charles Briggs of the 319th Squadron said. "Just drop us a marker."

A moment later, the bombardier on Ekstrand's lead plane, using H2X radar, dropped a green pathfinder flare and then released his bombs from the aircraft. A few bombs hit some oil storage tanks near the village of Semoi. But because of the heavy cloud cover, the 90th Group airmen could not see the results clearly, although they did note two huge fires. The other 90th Group squadrons bombed the Samarinda airstrip east of Manggar Field and punched huge holes in the runway, while destroying four parked transport planes along the runway. The fourth Jolly Roger squadron bombed the dock area on Balikpapan Bay and destroyed at least two piers along with several barges.

The FEAF bombers had droned over Balikpapan for more than an hour before the last bomb fell at 1042. But as the B-24s circled over the area and climbed to 20,000 feet to start for home, Anabuki mustered his pilots and zoomed after the Americans. Over Makassar Strait, the Japanese pressed a new attack against the American formations. In fact, even AA fire from ships in Balikpapan Harbor lashed out at the departing U.S. planes.

The American gunners of the 5th Bomb Group fired at the attacking Zeros and Oscars of the 381st Sentai. But the Japanese now took a toll. Anabuki himself caught A/C 932 with several 20mm hits that tore off two engines and a wing. The big Liberator keeled over and fell into Balikpapan Bay. Fellow Bomber Baron airmen saw no parachutes and they could only assume that all 10 crew members were gone. Kuroe and the pilots of his flight hit A/C 529 and 260 with an array of 7.7. tracer fire and 20mm shells. The heavy fusillade tore both planes apart. All hands on A/C 529 were killed as the plane crashed into Makassar Strait. However, the pilot of A/C 260 managed to ditch his plane and, remarkably, a PBY rescued all crew members.

The 5th Group also suffered serious damage to 13 more B-24s from the determined interceptor pilots and AA gunners. Some aircraft lost engines; others had tails, wings, and fuselages punched full of holes. A few lost hydraulic systems, radio equipment, or navigational gear. More than 50 crew members aboard the 5th Group planes were killed and another 50 wounded, not counting those who had been lost on the downed Bomber Baron B-24s.

In the 307th Group, the B-24s astonishingly suffered little loss. Several planes received minor damage and two planes sustained serious damage. Further, besides the Japanese planes downed by Sgts. Black and O'Brien, Sgt. Sam Leffort and Sgt. Ed Anderson aboard Colonel Burnham's plane had also downed one interceptor each. Other Long Ranger gunners had downed two more enemy planes and scored two probables.

The 90th Bomb Group had also taken losses. Lieutenant Anabuki's unit aggressively jumped this last formation of FEAF bombers, riddling one plane and sending it into Makassar Strait. Crews aboard other Jolly Roger planes heard SOS signals and saw yellow objects on the water which resembled life rafts. And in fact, the crew on the downed A/C 3965 Jolly Roger plane was rescued, save for one man.

The Jolly Rogers suffered considerable damage to eight more of their aircraft with 37 crewmen killed and 52 wounded. During the return flight from Balikpapan, no less than 30 to 40 interceptors had jumped them. But, on Maj. Vern Ekstrand's plane, gunners Al Tulley and Frank Gutierre ganged up on an Oscar and blew the Japanese plane to pieces.

Another consolation for the Jolly Rogers was Sgt. Steve Novak aboard Maj. Charles Briggs' *Phyliss J. of Worcester*. Novak caught one Zeke with withering fire and disintegrated the Japanese fighter. He also damaged a second interceptor, sending the plane wobbling off with a trail of smoke as a probable kill. On the same plane, Gunner Harry Clay also downed an Oscar fighter plane.

Still, Anabuki and his pilots chased the B-24s eastward for 240 miles, while they made at least 70 more passes against the 5th Group Liberators alone. The Japanese finally broke off their attacks when the B-24s got too far west and the 381st Sentai pilots needed to come home. The Japanese had scored four kills and severely damaged many other Liberators. Further, they had killed or wounded scores of FEAF airmen. In turn, the B-24 gunners had claimed a total of ten fighters down and at least a dozen more damaged.

As the battered American formation headed east, many of the pilots aboard damaged aircraft feared they would not get home. Fortunately, as they reached the Celebes, they again ran into heavy clouds, one to two miles deep, and Musgrave once again drove his B-24s into the thick banks to avoid Japanese 382nd Sentai and 22nd Kokutai interceptors that came out of Manado and Kendari for the second time that day.

But as the B-24s droned over the Molucca Sea, the skies cleared and Col. Tom Musgrave feared that interceptors might rise from Bitjoli to jump his formation. He recklessly broke radio silence and called FEAF headquarters in Noemfoor.

"We're in tough shape," the 5th Bomb Group commander said. "We've got a lot of cripples coming home. If we get jumped over the Halmaheras, half of us may not get home. Can we have some fighter cover?"

"You got it, Colonel," the ADVON aide said.

Gen. St. Clair Streett had anticipated just such a problem and he had kept a squadron of P47s from the U.S. 49th Fighter Group on stand by alert at Cape Sansapor. FEAF immediately called the base and within moments, 22 Thunderbolts under Maj. Wallace Jordan of the group's 9th Squadron zoomed off the strip and sped westward to the Halmaheras to meet the returning B-24s. The Liberators had just crossed the west coast of the island when Tom Musgrave and Fred Bonds saw the planes ahead.

"Holy Christ, more bandits!" the bombardier cried.

"No, I think they're P-47s," Musgrave answered.

Several minutes later, the 22 American fighter planes reached the B-24s and immediately ringed the big U.S. bombers.

"Okay, Colonel, we're with you," Major Jordan said. "If Nip interceptors come out of Bitjoli or Ambiona, we'll take care of them."

"God, are we glad to see you," Musgrave said.

Aboard the B-24s, crew members ogled the P-47s men as though they had just been plucked to safety from the mouth of an erupting volcano: gunners Jim Shaw, Merv Anderson, Harold Trout, Joe Tribble, Charlie Smith, Hal Phillips, Chuck Lee and Wes Barker of the 5th Group; gunners Sam Leffort, Ed Anderson, Ralph O'Brien, and Joe Black of the 307th; and gunners like Steve Novak, Harry Clay, Frank Gutierre, and Al Tulley of the 90th. Their .50 caliber barrels were blistering hot, their ammo belts all but empty, and their nerves in knots. These gunners were in no condition to fight off another swarm of Japanese fighter planes.

Soon enough, 20 planes from Bitjoli zoomed south to attack the American bombers. However, Lt. Commander Tanaka and his navy pilots from the 19th Kokutai were no match for the American fighter pilots. Before the Japanese planes had come within ten miles of the Liberators, the P-47 airmen shot down three of the Oscars and damaged four more. The shocked Tanaka quickly broke off and fled back to Bitjoli. Major Jordan followed the Japanese planes for several minutes, but he then called off the pursuit, much to the disappointment of his 9th Squadron pilots. However, Jordan's job was to escort the B-24s home.

By 1600 hours, the Liberators finally reached Noemfoor and landed one by one on the Kornaseron strip. Many of the planes were damaged, with some bellying in, others plowing off the runway, and two coming down with feathered props. Medics hurried to an array of planes to extricate hordes of wounded from the battered craft, and they hurried these injured to aid stations.

The ground crews watched the activities soberly for their worst fears had materialized. On this mission to Balikpapan, the bomber crews had endured a nightmare. But even more ominous—the air crews would soon return to this distant target, and again without fighter escorts.

Chapter Seven

When the crews of the 5th Bomb Group reported to operations for post mission reports, Capt. William Stewart and his operations staff passed out shots of Hiram Walker whiskey to each man. The whiskey allotment after a bombing raid had become standard routine designed to calm the combat airman's nerves. The shots did not really calm anyone and in reality, the liquor ration was more of a reward than a dose of medicine. Most of the Bomber Baron airmen still trembled from the traumatic, long distance flight even after they downed their whiskey. Some crewmen even shunned their rations and passed them on to fellow airmen.

The men sitting on the benches in front of the operations tent podium had diminished in number because 70 crew members who had sat here 15 hours ago had not returned. One entire crew was missing, another 30 had been killed by Japanese interceptor pilots or AA fire, and 29 wounded had been whisked off to the Noemfoor base hospital.

"I know you had tough opposition today and you're not in the mood for giving reports," Stewart said, "but still, we need to get an idea of what happened."

Col. Tom Musgrave, Maj. James Pierce, and other squadron or flight leaders responded positively to the operations staff. Extensive damage had been done to the Pandansari refinery, the airmen said, although they could not get a clear view of damage because of heavy smoke, fire, and cloud cover.

"I'm sure we put the refinery out of business," Musgrave said.

Captain Stewart nodded and then elicited reports on casualties. The group had lost three B-24s. A/C 932 was shot down over target with all hands missing in action and presumed dead. A/C 529 and A/C 260 had also been abandoned because of battle damage. The crew of A/C 529 was apparently lost since no parachutes were seen coming out of the plane that had exploded in midair. However, observers were certain that the PBY had rescued at least some of Lieutenant Egleston's crew on A/C 260.

Egleston's plane had lost its No. 1 engine and he had brought the plane to a position of 0 degrees by 120 degrees before ordering the crew to bail out. Seven men and one life raft had parachuted into the water from 1500 feet. Then Egleston had gained altitude and at 2,000 feet three more men had parachuted to the water before the plane crashed into the sea and burned about 2,000 yards from the PBY rescue plane. Three aircraft had circled the area and dropped more rafts and water markers. When last seen the Catalina was on the water and taxiing toward the downed aircraft's survivors.

The group had also suffered serious damage to 13 planes. Two of them had made emergency landings at Morotai and three at Cape Sansapor, with most of these five planes carrying some dead or wounded aboard. The crew on board A/C 591 had made it back to Noemfoor. However, in order to lighten load, the crew had thrown out all remaining ammunition, two waist guns, part of the nose guns, the complete ball turret, all flak suits and helmets, and some radio equipment. Other aircraft returning to Noemfoor had also suffered an array of damage, loss of life, and numerous wounded.

The 5th Bomb Group gunners had claimed four enemy planes down, three kills from the gunners aboard Musgrave's plane: Sgt. Harold Trout, Sgt. Marv Anderson, and Sgt. Jim Shaw. They had also claimed seven Japanese interceptors probably destroyed.

When Stewart finished interrogating crew members in the operations tent, he gestured to the men. "I guess we've got all the information. Try to rest up awhile before evening chow. You've had a long day."

"You're dismissed," Colonel Musgrave said.

The men shuffled off in near silence for most of them were too tired and spent to do much talking. Gunners Jim Shaw, Marv Anderson, and Harold Trout were too depressed over today's losses to discuss their kills against Japanese fighter planes. They ambled to their tent quarters and sacked out, falling to sleep almost at once. Sgt. Joe Tribble, Charlie Smith, and Hal Phillips felt equally drained and they said little to ground crews about the enemy planes they had shot down. Gunners Charlie Lee and Wes Barker took invigorating showers in the outdoor facilities, grateful to be alive. Lt. Jim Russell and Lt. Ken Gutheil ambled to the officers mess for coffee, while Col. Tom Musgrave, Maj. Al James, Maj. Jim Pierce, and other squadron leaders walked off to their quarters to rest before evening chow.

A mile away, at the 307th Bomb Group campsite,

Col. Bob Burnham also held a post mission briefing. His crews were not as somber as the airmen of the 5th Group, for the Long Rangers had been the most fortunate of the three heavy bomb groups which had hit Balikpapan. In fact, the gunners chattered eagerly over their exploits of downing four enemy planes, one each by Sgts. Sam Leffort. Ed Anderson, Joe Black, and Ralph O'Brien, while other gunners had scored five probable kills.

On this mission, the 307th had suffered only minor damage to a pair of B-24s. One bomber had sustained damage to the hydraulic and pilot systems from 20mm shell fire. The other B-24 had received minor damage from an AA burst. Remarkably, the Long Rangers had not lost a single man killed nor a crew member seriously wounded. And more astonishingly, the enemy tactic of dropping phosphorous bombs from above the 307th formation had proven utterly fruitless, while the gunners aboard the Liberators had damaged some of the enemy planes dropping the phosphorous bombs.

The 307th had expended 230x250 bombs over Balikpapan and they had used up 8,000 rounds of ammunition against interceptors. Meanwhile, using H2X radar, the bombers from the lead 372nd Squadron had claimed serious hits on the Pandansari refinery in their bomb drops. The other squadrons had claimed serious damage on the paraffin-lube plant and other installations in and about the huge oil complex.

"We were goddamn lucky compared to the other groups," Bob Burnham told his operations staff. "We got intercepted by twenty or thirty enemy planes but apparently they got a little squeamish after their clash with the 5th Bomb Group gunners. We were also fortunate to escape serious AA damage."

"Yes sir," the operations officer said.

"Is there anything else you need?" Musgrave asked the operations officer.

"No sir."

Musgrave nodded and then looked at his combat crews. "No doubt we'll be going back to Balikpapan, since we've only begun this job on the refineries. But, for the moment, get some rest and stay loose."

"Yes, sir," Lt. Don Forke said.

"When do you think we'll go back, sir?" Lieutenant Covington asked.

"That'll be up to General Streett," Burnham said. "I'll guess they'll send recon planes over that refinery complex and get a look at the damage we did before they make out a new field order." He paused and spoke again. "Any questions?"

"None."

"Okay, you're dismissed," the colonel gestured.

For the 90th Bomb Group, the crewmen only enjoyed an hour's rest at Noemfoor while ordnance men gassed up their aircraft. Then, the Jolly Roger B-24s took off and flew on to their Mokmer Drome on Biak Island, arriving there shortly before dusk. They had been away from their campsites for 18 hours, so it had been a long day. Maj. Vern Ekstrand, who had led the Jolly Roger formation, allowed his crew members to clean up and eat evening chow before he called them into a post mission briefing. These men too got their shots of Hiram Walker to supposedly calm their nerves. However, the shots were merely routine. If the whiskey had been truly for medicinal purposes, the men should have gotten their alcoholic drinks when they first landed in Noemfoor three hours ago.

After the rounds of whiskey, the operations officer, Capt. Greg Smith, questioned the Jolly Roger airmen to complete post mission reports. The 90th had come in behind the 5th and 307th, crossed the Borneo coast just above Manggar runway, made a 275 degree turn, and had then headed for target—the Edeleanu sulfuric acid plant. But the target had been so heavily covered with dense clouds that bombardiers could not find the plant. So, the B-24s of the 90th had dropped a total of 136x250 pound bombs on other targets, including oil storage tanks near the village of Semoi.

As to losses, one 90th Group B-24 had gone down, but its crew had been rescued by a PBY. However, like the 5th Group, the Jolly Rogers had also counted a large number of dead and wounded aboard their eight seriously damaged aircraft. The 52 wounded had been left behind at Noemfoor for treatment at the island's base hospital, while the B-24s had carried back to Biak their 37 dead who would be tagged by graves registration teams before burial.

"I don't know when we'll go out again," Major Ekstrand told his bomber crews, "but I suspect it may be within the next two or three days. We haven't even begun to finish off that oil target. Meanwhile, get some rest. We'll have our ground crews make repairs on damaged planes, but maybe they'll need to junk some of them."

When operations officer Greg Smith got all his information, he gestured to the crewmen. "Thank you for your patience and help."

Maj. Charles Briggs, Lt. Hank Pennington, Lt.

General Douglas MacArthur (L), CinC of SWPA, and General George Kenney (C) discuss Balikpapan air raid strategy with SWPA staff.

General St. Clair Streett, CO of the 13th Air Force, was the OTC for the Balikpapan air campaign.

Col. Tom Musgrave led the 5th Bomb Group on all five missions to Balikpapan.

Sgt. Joe Tribble, a gunner aboard 5th Group B-24, fought off hordes of Japanese interceptors to save their Liberator.

Sgt. Chuck Lee, aboard Lt. Gutheil's Blackjack, *downed one Zero and damaged a second.*

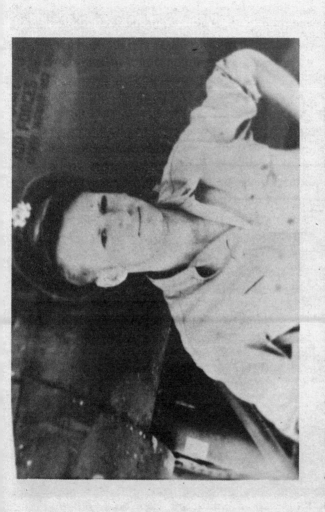

Col. Bob Burnham, CO of the 307th Bomb Group led his bombers against Balikpapan on all five raids.

Sgt. Joe Black, a 307th Group waist gunner-radio operation, shot down two interceptors.

Lt. Don Forke of the 307th Bomb Group, also participated in all five dangerous missions to the Borneo oil complex.

Sgt. Ralph O'Brien (R), a gunner on Forke's plane, shot down two Japanese planes.

Major Vern Ekstrand of the 90th Bomb Group led his unit on three of the raids and scored heavily against the refineries.

Woody Keefe

Major Charles Briggs of 90th Group (L) gets his major leaf pinned on him byhis co-pilot, Lt. Hank Pennington. Briggs led the Jolly Roger 319th Squadron.

Sgt. Steve Novak, a gunner on Major Briggs' B-24, got himself three kills during the Balikpapan air campaign.

Major Charles King led the two fighter squadrons of the 35th Fighter Group on the longest fighter plane flight ever during the Balikpapan air campaign.

Lt. Bob Johnson of the 41st Squadron got himself two Zeros. In fact 35th Group pilots knocked down almost 60 Japanese planes during the air campaign.

Major Wallace Jordan of the 9th Headhunter Squadron took on Japanese fighter units that outnumbered him, but he and his pilots scored heavily.

Major Richard Bong, supposedly retired from combat, joined the 9th Squadron in the Balikpapan raids and scored three kills.

Major Jay Robbins of the 8th Fighter Group, macerated a Japanese Kokutai unit that tried to intercept the B-24 bombers on the fourth Balikpapan raid.

General Soemu Anami, CinC of the Japanese 2nd Area Forces, planned a defense against possible American attacks on the Balikpapan refineries.

Gen. Shosho Ichanbangese, CinC of the Makassar Base Force, had the responsibility of carrying out the defensive measures at Balikpapan.

Admiral Mitsuo Fuchida, CO of the 4th Air Fleet, was responsible for the air defense of the East Indies. His air units failed miserably.

Col. Maseo Matsumae, CO of the 7th Air Division, was severely reprimanded because his Sentai pilots failed to stop the Americans.

Lt. Satoshi Anabuki led the 381st Sentai in defense of Balikpapan, but he failed.

Lt. Masauyki Nakase and some of his pilots of the 381st Sentai in the Celebes. They could not stop the Americans from flying to Balikpapan.

Captain Sonokawa of the 23rd Air Flotilla was also reprimanded because his naval pilots also failed to stop the Americans.

Cmdr. Joyotara Iwami of the 22nd Kokutai saw his air unit cut to pieces by U.S. army fighter pilots as U.S. navy pilots had cut his unit to pieces in the Marianas fight.

Ens. Susumu Ishihara (lower right) and pilots of the 22nd Sentai. They proved totally inadequate against American fighter pilots.

Lt. Cmdr. Nobuo Fujita of the 20th Sentai at Balikpapan failed to stop any of the Liberator bombing attacks.

Captain Zenji Orita of submarine I-176 patrolled the East Indies waters. He gave Japanese air units plenty of warning about approaching American planes.

Beautiful downtown Balikpapan in a 1942 photo.

The cracking plant of the Balikpapan refineries; photo taken in 1942.

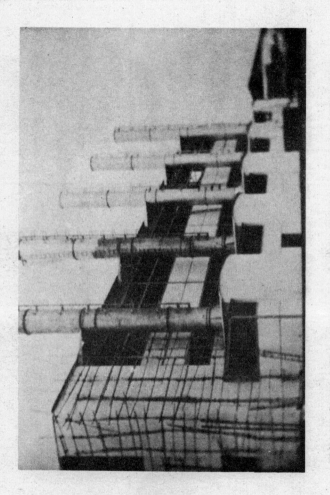

The Edeleanu sulfuric acid plant of the refineries; photo taken in 1942.

A B-24 takes off from Noemfoor for long 1100 mile flight to Balikpapan.

A B-24 drops its bombs on the Balikpapan refineries.

B-24s of the 307th Bomb Group wing above the clouds on the way to Borneo.

Massive attack on Balikpapan refineries sends smoke rising more than 6,000 feet into the air.

5th Bomb Group planes strike the Edeleanu plant squarely during attack.

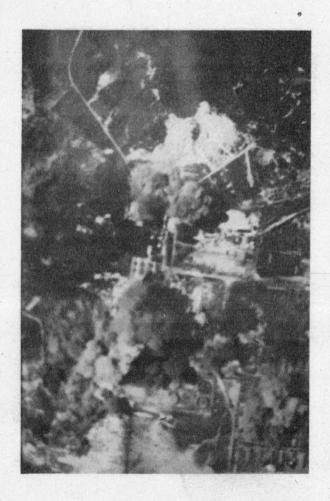

90th Bomb Group B24s also hit their target squarely during Balikpapan raid.

10-10-44
22nd GP.

[PRESERVE?] REFINERY

14-10-44
22nd GP.
43rd GP.
90th. GP.

Recon photos by U.S. PBY snooper planes show damage to the Balikpapan refineries following the 10 October 1944 raid.

Tom Glassman, Lt. Frank Mann, Lt. Al Rehm, and other officers ambled off to the officers mess to drink coffee, while enlisted men for the most part walked off to their tent quarters to sleep. Gunners like Steve Novak, Harry Clay, Al Tulley, and Frank Gutierre were simply too tired to indulge in bull sessions or to discuss their exploits. They fell asleep almost at once. They could talk about their downed enemy planes tomorrow, when they were rested and when the trauma of losing so many comrades had abated somewhat.

At his 13th Air Force ADVON headquarters at Noemfoor, Gen. St. Clair Streett was still awake at midnight, studying copies of the after action reports that had come to his office from the three bomb groups. He was quite dismayed over the loss of four big bombers, the damage to so many more B-24s, and the large number of dead and wounded. He could not recall when heavy bomber groups had taken such a beating on a SWPA combat mission. Still, he could not suspend the air operations against Balikpapan. When he finished reading the reports he turned to his operations chief, Col. John Murtha.

"I want PBYs out right after midnight to get a good look at the damage we did today. If possible, I want both visual and photographic assessments. We'll need to study recon reports before we prepare the next FO to Balikpapan. If snooper reports have been evaluated by tomorrow evening, we can send out the B-24s in a day or two. We don't want to give the Nips time to make repairs before we hit them again."

"No sir," Murtha said.

By the evening of 29 September, bustling activity

prevailed at Balikpapan. Gen. Shosho Ichabangese had put to work every available Japanese soldier and airman to snuff out fires, clear debris, make repairs, and fill the bomb craters at the Samarinda airstrip. The Makassar Base Force commander had also commandeered every Chinese coolie worker and Indonesian civilian he could find to repair damage to barracks, harbor piers, and ruptured fuel lines. He then called General Anami at the 2nd Area Forces headquarters in Kudat, Borneo, to report the results of the U.S. air attack.

"I regret to say, Honorable Anami," Ichabangese said, "that neither the 381st Sentai nor the 246th Anti-aircraft Battalion were able to prevent the Yankee air bombardment. However, these pilots and gunners destroyed or damaged at least half of the attacking bombers. I can tell you that we are working without rest to repair damage."

"I will fly to Balikpapan at once," Anami said, "and bring Colonel Matsumae with me. I will also ask Admiral Fuchida to fly down from his headquarters in Singapore."

"Yes, Honorable Anami."

By the late afternoon of 30 September, General Anami and Colonel Matsumae of the 7th Air Division had arrived at Balikpapan from Kudat, and the two men personally surveyed the results of the American air raids. They also spoke to the refinery supervisor and the Makassar Base Force maintenance officer. The two visitors then ate an evening meal with General Ichabangese, Major Magari, Lieutenant Anabuki, and Lt. Commander Fujita who had now arrived at Balikpapan to prepare his 20th Naval Kokutai for combat.

At 1900 hours the Japanese officers retired to the conference room of the Makassar Base Force headquarters. "I have spoken to those officers who were in the best position to assess damage," Anami said. "We were told that the main Pandansari refinery plant has been one third destroyed, but they can still operate at fifty percent capacity. The paraffin plant has been seriously damaged, but can still operate at ninety percent capacity. Fortunately, the cracking plant, Edeleanu plant, boiler and treatment houses, and the Manggar airfield have not been damaged. However, we did lose three vessels in the harbor, four aircraft at Samarinda Field, and two oil storage tanks. We also suffered damage to the coolie barracks, some pipelines, and a power station."

Anami paused and then continued. "I am pleased to note, however, that General Ichabangese wasted no time in putting to work every available man to make repairs. Within a day or two, he should have all systems back to normal. I appreciate your quick action, General."

"Thank you," Ichabangese said.

"Yes," Anami gestured, "we would be naive indeed to think the Americans will not return again with their heavy bombers. If they flew to Balikpapan today, they can fly here tomorrow, and the next day, and the next week. The enemy's long range reconnaissance planes have already been over Balikpapan to study the damage by their bombers. We must be prepared to meet these Yankee intruders again. The interceptor

114

pilots must improve their efforts," the general said to Colonel Matsumae.

The 7th Air Division commander responded by half scowling at Anabuki. "I had hoped, Lieutenant, that you and your pilots of the 381st Sentai might have stopped these enemy bombers."

"We did what we could," Lieutenant Anbauki answered. "They had more heavy bombers than we had fighter aircraft, and these huge B-24s carry a large number of guns, at least a dozen on each aircraft. Pilots destroyed or damaged at least half of this enemy formation and no doubt badly hurt the aim of their bombardiers. Otherwise, the Americans would have surely caused more damage than they did."

"I must agree with Lieutenant Anabuki," Lt. Commander Fujita suddenly spoke. "I believe that the 381st Sentai pilots are to be congratulated for their efforts."

Col. Matsumae merely grunted.

"And what of the anti-aircraft batteries?" General Anami asked. "Why were they not more effective?"

"We did not have all guns in place, Honorable General," Major Magari said. "Unfortunately, the enemy attack on the harbor shipping a few days ago badly disrupted the unloading process and caused considerable delay. However we are working without rest and by tomorrow evening every one of our thirty anti-aircraft guns will be ready."

"Good," General Anami said. "I doubt if the American bombers will be here again for at least two or three days. As is their custom, they will want to study reconnaissance reports thoroughly before they make new attacks. This is especially true of a target that lies so far from their home base." He then looked at Lt. Commander Fujita. "And what of your naval kokutai?"

"Our fighter planes will be here in the morning and we will base these fifty aircraft at Samarinda Drome. It is my understanding that the field will be repaired by morning."

"All will be ready by then, Commander," General Ichabangese said. "Your aircraft will have no difficulty in landing."

"Captain Sonakawa regrets that he could not attend this meeting," Lt. Commander Fujita said, "but he is conducting his own conference with the 23rd Air Flotilla and 7th Air Division at Kendari in the Celebes. The honorable captain is planning new, coordinated systems of attacks along the potential route followed by the American formations from their New Guinea bases. Captain Sonokawa regrets his failure to intercept the enemy aircraft today. However, our pilots in the Halmaheras were hindered by darkness and our pilots in the Celebes were foiled by thick cloud covers. Captain Sonokawa hopes they will not be so unfortunate the next time."

"Good," General Anami nodded. He then sighed, "It appears we have covered all possibilities and we can now end this conference. I must emphasize again, however, that we must be alert and resolute. Major," he pointed to Magari, "be sure that your anti-aircraft gunners are in position with plenty of ammunition at all times."

"Yes, Honorable General."

"As for you air commanders," the 2nd Area Forces CinC shuttled his glance between Anabuki and Fujita,

116

"be sure that your pilots in the future act with courage and with aggression. You have well over one hundred aircraft between your two air units and you should be able to deal effectively with any new enemy air attacks."

"Yes, Honorable General," Lieutenant Anabuki said.

The evening did not pass quietly at Balikpapan because Japanese soldiers, Nippon airmen, Chinese coolies, and Indonesian civilians worked tirelessly to repair damage in and about the refineries. By daylight they had made good progress.

At 0600 hours, 1 October, however, the air raid sirens wailed through Balikpapan and the surrounding countryside. Indonesian civilians hurried from their varied tasks to seek cover. Most of them grumbled about a new air attack only 48 hours after the last one. Many of them grumbled at this atmosphere of war which had replaced the placid life at their beautiful city on Borneo's east coast. They knew the Americans were after the refineries, but errant bombs had fallen elsewhere on the 29 September raid and the same could happen again today.

However, no American bombers were overhead. Instead, only a single interloper, another high flying PBY reconnaissance plane, droned across the sky. The U.S. aircraft flew at 25,000 feet, well above the range of Japanese anti-aircraft guns. The Catalina was making another visual and photographic assessment of the Balikpapan refineries. By the time the Japanese sent up interceptors to shoot down the American snooper, the Catalina was long gone.

By dark of 1 October, the PBY reached Noemfoor Island in Geelvink Bay and lab men quickly developed the photos, while G-2 quickly evaluated the statements from visual observers.

At 1700 hours, Gen. St. Clair Streett and his 13th Air Force staff were studying the reports and the photographs. "This is good stuff," Colonel Murtha said, "even if it isn't too encouraging."

"Well," Streett answered, "at least we know exactly where we stand. We apparently did considerable damage to the Pandansari refinery, but we didn't knock it out altogether, and we only did minor damage to the paraffin plant. We didn't even touch the cracking plant, the Edeleanu sulfuric acid plant, or the boiler house and water treatment plant."

Col. Murtha nodded. "The photographs also indicate that the Japanese have worked hard to repair damage."

"We'll launch our next air attack as soon as possible," Streett said. "MacArthur is getting restless."

"Yes sir."

"The Nips are making elaborate defense preparations in the Philippines. They're mustering a battleship flotilla, a carrier fleet, a horde of planes, and plenty of men and armor. The enemy will need fuel from Balikpapan to run that war machine, so MacArthur wants that refinery complex smashed before he lands in the Philippines. The invasion of Leyte is set for about three weeks from today. What's the weather forecast for the Indies?"

"There could be a cloud front closing in now," the officer answered. "The PBY was lucky to get over Borneo before the front closed in. Meteorologists say the front will take a couple of days to pass and then the skies are expected to clear."

Streett sighed. "Okay, then we'll plan the next attack on Balikpapan two days from now. How about 3 October?"

"That should be fine," Murtha nodded.

"We'll draw up an FO in the morning for the 5th and 307th Groups. I want to hit the Pandansari refinery again, the cracking plant, and the sulfuric acid plant. The two groups will mount as many bombers as they can."

"It's too bad they don't have fighter escort," Murtha said. "It would make their job a hell of a lot easier."

"General McMullen is trying to work out something in the way of dual auxiliary tanks on our fighter planes," the 13th Air Force commander said. "But, we can't wait. The 5th and 307th must go out again quickly. Tell Colonel Musgrave and Colonel Burnham to ready their planes and crews."

"Yes sir," Murtha answered.

Chapter Eight

At 0200 hours, 3 October, Col. Bob Burnham sat in the lead B-24 of his 307th Bomb Group. The moon, high and bright to the south, reflected silvery sparkles off the cockpit windows of the big Liberator. Burnham was not as tense this evening as he had been on the evening of 29 September. The first strike against Balikpapan, even without escorts, had not hurt him too badly, although the intercepting Japanese pilots had badly macerated the 5th and 90th Bomb Groups, while his B-24 gunners had done well against the enemy pilots.

Next to Burnham, co-pilot Joe Rodrick sat quietly, watching the control tower at the far end of Kornaseron Drome. He also glanced to his right where Lt. Don Forke sat waiting in his own B-24. Rodrick jerked when Colonel Burnham picked up his intercom and called his other crewmen.

"Navigator, is everything okay?"

"Yes sir."

"Bombardier?"

"All set, sir," Lieutenant Brown answered.

"Gunners?"

The five gunners, including the engineer gunner, left and right waist gunners, belly gunner, turret gunner, and tail gunner, also answered in the positive. Their guns were working and their machine gun belts were full.

Thus the other eight men of the B-24 crew were ready. The colonel, however, felt distressed over one factor: the long 12 to 14 hour flight that would tire his crew and erode their effectiveness. Still, he had relished the first attack on the Balikpapan refineries, the lustiest target he had ever hit during his Pacific combat.

Finally, the green light blinked from the control tower. Burnham revved the four big engines of his B-24 and then roared down the Kornaseron runway with his wingman, Don Forke, at his side. A moment later, the heavily laden Liberator rose skyward and banked northward out to sea. Within five minutes, 22 other heavily laden B-24s also rose upward and headed out to sea.

As the 307th circled in the sky to merge into formation, the fat bellied Liberators of the 5th Bomb Group lumbered towards the head of the runway like lazy, pregnant dinosaurs. The roar of the hundred big engines echoed across the level terrain of Noemfoor Island with a deafening din. Ground crews about the field winced from the screaming props that pierced the eardrums, and they cowered from the streaming, ashen dust that shot across the flats.

At 0215 hours, Col. Tom Musgrave wheeled into the head of the runway with his wingman Ken Gutheil at his side. Musgrave too called his gunners, navigator, radio man, and bombardier to make certain they were set and ready for the long flight to Balikpapan. Then, at 0227, the light once more blinked green from the control tower. Musgrave revved his four engines, released the brakes, and then roared down the runway in unison with Ken Gutheil.

Soon, 18 more Liberators raced down the runway, using most of the 8,000 feet length before rising upward with their heavy loads.

By 0245 hours, the 44 Liberators from the 13th Air Force had jelled into tight four-plane boxes and headed west by northwest over the Vogelkop Peninsula. By 0330, the B-24s were droning over the fighter base at Sansapor, the most forward airfield of the Far East Air Forces. The roars awoke some of the airmen of the 49th Fighter Group who squinted up at the dark shapes of American bombers as the B-24s droned westward. These men felt a pang of sympathy for the 13th Air Force crews. The B-24 airmen should have had escorts for the long mission, but no P-47 at Sansapor could possibly make the 936 mile flight to Balikpapan.

Soon, the B-24s were over the open sea west of New Guinea. As the Liberators neared Djailalo Passage, east of the Halmaheras, Bob Burnham picked up his intercom and called his crew. "We're approaching the southern tip of Halmahera. Gunners stay alert! Stay alert. We might get night fighter bandits out of Bitjoli."

"Yes sir," somebody answered.

But the B-24 crossed the tip of the island and headed into the Molucca Sea without any Japanese planes coming south to intercept the Americans. Burnham sighed in relief. They had crossed their first hurdle without incident. If the rest of the flight was equally uneventful, he and his bomber crews might enjoy a milk run.

However, the Japanese were waiting.

Capt. Zenji Orita, in submarine I-176, had been patrolling just north of Mangole Island, in the south sector of the Molucca Sea. Radar men in the radio room caught blips on the screen and they guessed at once that the big U.S. B-24s were again heading into the Indies. They quickly called the 1st Submarine Squadron commander in the I-Boat's control room.

"Enemy bombers are flying due west."

"How many?"

"Perhaps forty or fifty of them."

"Bakyra!" Orita cried. The Americans were obviously on the way to Balikpapan again. He quickly charted the position of the U.S. planes at about 126° west by 2° south. The captain then sent a coded message to Kendari. "Enemy bombers flying westward with probable target of Balikpapan."

The 13th Air Force B-24s were still a long way from target, so the Japanese had plenty of time to send out interceptors. Unfortunately for the Americans, aggressive Nippon pilots had taken up stations in both the Celebes and in Balikpapan itself. The B-24s would be crossing the Celebes at just about daybreak so the interceptors could attack them. And, in fact, Cmdr. Joyotara Iwami had his airmen of the 22nd Kokutai on full alert. As soon as the coded message reached Kendari from Captain Orita's I-176, the veteran of the Battle of the Philippine Sea alerted his pilots to action. Iwami hoped to avenge the terrible Japanese aerial defeat during the Mariana Turkey Shoot in June.

By 0500 hours, Iwami was airborne with 24 Oscars from the 22nd Kokutai. 24 Zeros from the 382nd Sentai under Lieutenant Nakase had taken off from

Manado in the northern Celebes to also intercept the Americans. Meanwhile, at Balikpapan, Lt. Commander Fujita and Lieutenant Anabuki quickly mustered the fighter pilots of the 381st Sentai and 20th Kokutai. About 48 army and navy Oscars, Tonys, and Zeros would take off as soon as the American bombers entered Makassar Strait between the Celebes and Borneo. The Balikpapan pilots would jump any U.S. planes which escaped the Celebes air units.

At 0630 hours, four hours after leaving Noemfoor, the 44 B-24s were droning over the Tomini Gulf in the Celebes before crossing the island's northwest isthmus and then heading over Makassar Strait to Balikpapan. But at 0635 hours, waist gunner Sam Leffort on Col. Bob Burnham's lead B-24 spotted the swarm of planes to the south—the 24 Japanese fighters from Kendari under Commander Iwami.

"Bandits at nine o'clock! Nine o'clock!"

Bob Burnham squinted from his cockpit window and saw the approaching Japanese fighter planes himself. He quickly called his crew. "Bandits at nine o'clock, high; nine o'clock high! Tighten formation. Gunners, stay alert. Fire as soon as they come into range."

In his own B-24, Lt. Don Forke craned his neck and peered out of his cockpit until he too saw the approaching enemy fighter planes. He quickly called his gunners on the intercom. "Here they come! Get ready to fire!"

Meanwhile, Commander Iwami peered from the cockpit of his lead Oscar. When he came within two miles of the tight American formations, he called his pilots. "We will attack from three o'clock in pairs; in pairs. Lieutenant Ishihara's unit will climb above the enemy bombers to drop phosphorous bombs."

"Yes, Commander," Susumu Ishihara answered.

Moments later, the Japanese pilots roared into the American bombers, spitting chattering 7.7 machine gun fire and whooshing 20mm shells at the fat bellied Liberators. American gunners, meanwhile, swung turret, belly, and waist guns at the Japanese planes, unleashing streams of .50 caliber machine gun fire. The sky trembled from the heavy exchange that echoed across the gulf like a staccato of thunder.

The first diamond of four Liberators caught withering machine gun fire as the Oscars made several passes in two plane attacks. About 20 7.7mm hits tattooed the wing and fuselage of Burnham's lead plane, forcing him and his co-pilot to cover instinctively. The hits opened holes in the fuselage and cold, heavy blasts rushed inside the plane and struck the waist gunners like multiple streams of arctic air at this 16,000 feet altitude. Sergeant Leffort and his fellow gunners wrapped their heavy furlined jackets around them tighter and they pulled the fur lined gloves up to their wrists.

After the Oscar attack, Burnham called his crew. "Damage!" he cried. "What's the damage?"

"Okay in bombardier compartment," Lt. Wes Brown said.

"No damage in navigator area."

"Radio section okay."

"Nose gun okay," Sgt. Ed Anderson said.

"Tail section not hit."

"Holes in the fuselage," Sergeant Leffort said. "It's a little cold in here, but we haven't suffered serious damage."

"Stay awake, stay awake!" Burnham cried. Then, a few moments later: "Get ready! Here they come again!"

"They're coming in from nine o'clock, nine o'clock," Bombardier Les Brown cried from his compartment.

The chatter of machine gun fire from several Oscars again pelted Burnham's plane and the big Liberator vibrated. This time, however, Sergeant Leffort and his left waist gunner scored solid hits on one of the Oscars. The engine of the enemy plane burst into flames before the Oscar tumbled head over tail and plopped into the gulf nearly three miles below. The fellow Oscar pilot also caught a barrage of hits and he arched away without damaging this lead aircraft of the 307th Group.

Lieutenant Ishihara and his wingman, who had already made two passes at the droning B-24s of the 307th Group, now came in again. This time they sent streams of 7.7mm machine gun fire at the tail end Liberator of the first diamond. Several slugs ripped into the bomb bay of A/C 933, piloted by Lt. Hange Gage. Steam and vapor erupted from the belly of the plane and the B-24 began losing altitude. Maj. Cliff Reese brought down his lead squadron plane to aid Gage, whose A/C 933 was now flying on three engines and carrying several wounded men aboard.

"Head for home," Major Reese cried.

"Yes sir," Gage answered.

But, as Gage turned away his damaged plane, Japanese fighters hit him again. Flames erupted from two more engines, the B-24 wobbled precariously eastward, dropped quickly in altitude, and then plopped into Tomini Gulf with all hands apparently lost.

The 22nd Kokutai continued to make more passes at the formation of B-24s. But even without escorts, the Liberators did enjoy some advantages. First, the big American bombers were huge and strong and they could take plenty of punishment from the Oscar 7.7mm rounds, even if such machine gun fire left many of the Liberators looking like sieves. Further, in their tight box formation, the B-24 gunners could shoot off a dozen or more guns from the left and right side, thus outgunning the eight guns of a pair of Oscars that attacked them. In fact, Oscar pilots had failed to down any more Liberators, although they did considerable damage to many of the 307th Group planes. In turn, the B-24 gunners knocked down three Oscars and damaged a dozen more, including a kill by Sgt. Ralph O'Brien aboard Lt. Don Forke's 307th Group Liberator.

But then, the flight of six Oscars above the formation of B-24s dropped their phosphorous bombs, intricately timed, so the bombs would explode at the same altitude at which the Liberators were flying. While most of these bombs exploded with terrible inaccuracy, two of them exploded against a Liberator of the 5th Bomb Group. The resulting blast ignited the B-24 and fires suddenly raged throughout the length of the Liberator. Most of the crew were seared into instant death, with only two men escaping the burning plane.

The flaming B-24 arced downward with trailing fire and smoke to crash into Tomini Gulf. Oscar pilots pounced on the two descending parachutes and killed both American airmen with rattling 7.7 wing fire. Lieutenant Ishihara did not scold his pilots, for the 22nd Kokutai flight leader understood the philosophy followed by Imperial Japanese Naval Headquarters: American airmen *must* be killed so they cannot fight another day.

By 0700 hours, the air battle was over. The Americans had lost two B-24s, suffered damage to four more that had to turn back, and lost about 40 airmen killed or wounded, including 20 killed from the two downed B-24s. The Japanese had lost five Oscars with damage to several more.

The Liberators had fortunately missed the 382nd Japanese army Sentai out of Manado. Lieutenant Nakase had arrived too late with his 23 fellow Zero pilots and he returned to base in disappointment.

But if the American airmen hoped their troubles had ended and they could now approach Balikpapan without further interception, they would be sadly disappointed. The surviving 38 B-24s, continuing to target, had cleared the Celebes isthmus west of Tomini Gulf and begun droning over Makassar Strait, the last leg of their journey, when they ran into more trouble.

As the U.S. bombers approached Balikpapan at 14,000 feet, a squadron of Oscars and Tonys from the 381st Sentai was already loitering at 18,000 feet. Lt. Satoshi Anabuki and his pilots hoped to make a better showing than they had on the first B-24 raid against Balikpapan.

Meanwhile, Lt. Cmdr. Nobuo Fujita roared off Samarinda Drome with 50 Zeros while Maj. Toshiro Magari's gunners had settled themselves into their gun pits and aimed 15 75mm and 15 90mm anti-aircraft guns skyward. They would unleash their flak as soon as they saw the first formation of American planes approaching Balikpapan.

At 0900 hours on this 3 October day, the air raid sirens again wailed through the streets of Balikpapan and the surrounding countryside. Residents once more scurried about in confusion and anger because it now appeared obvious that the Japanese could not prevent yet another air raid on their city.

Meanwhile, as the B-24s neared target, Lieutenant Anabuki called his pilots. "We will attack in pairs. In pairs! We will strike from nine and twelve o'clock." He then called Yashiko Kuroe. "You will take your flight and attack the second formation of enemy aircraft while we attack the lead formation. You and your pilots must harass them thoroughly. Even if you do not shoot down any of the big enemy bombers, you must keep them off balance and fearfully tense so that they cannot bomb with any degree of accuracy."

"I understand," F/O Kuroe said.

At 0917 hours, Sgt. Ed Anderson spotted the horde of Tony fighters to his left and he called Burnham. "Sir, bandits at nine o'clock."

The 307th Group colonel peered from his cockpit and cursed. "Son of a bitch, we got navy pilots, just like the ones at Rabaul. Those bastards can be a lot more aggressive than army pilots and they've got a lot more guns on those land based fighter planes. The bitches were waiting for us." He spoke quickly into his radio. "Gunners, stay alert! All crew members, stay alert! We're going to get hit hard, but we've come too far to turn back."

"In pairs, in pairs," Lt. Commander Fujita shouted again into his radio.

The Japanese naval pilots then swarmed into the American formations, unleashing streams of machine gun fire and whooshing 20mm cannon shells. But the American B-24 gunners were equally determined and they responded with their own withering .50 caliber fire from waists, bellies, and turret guns. The sky over Makassar Strait rumbled from the furious barrages as the Japanese fighters zoomed after the American bombers in pass after pass. But neither side could ward off the other, while both sides suffered losses.

307th Bomb Group gunners quickly downed several Oscars with their furious machine gun fire. Sgt. Joe Black got his second kill in two missions when he ripped off the wing of an Oscar before the plane fell like a limbless bird into the strait. Another Oscar had its engine chopped away and the Japanese plane dropped like a rock and plopped into the sea. From another B-24, .50 caliber fire shattered the cockpit of a Tony and splattered the pilot's head before the plane tumbled dizzily into the sea. A fourth plane, another Oscar, caught withering fire from belly and turret gunners after the Japanese pilot made his pass. The American gunners chopped off the tail of the enemy plane, which then plummeted out of sight.

Long Ranger gunners got another pair of Oscars almost simultaneously when streaming tracers shot away the wings and fuselages of both aircraft. Heavy smoke whooshed past the B-24s as the two 20th

Kokutai fighter planes spun downward and plopped into Makassar Strait.

But these victories by the American aerial gunners had not been without loss. Soon, the Japanese army and navy pilots from the 381st Sentai and 20th Kokutai took a murderous toll. Lt. Jim Wright, piloting the 307th Group's A/C 565, got jumped by seven Zeros that tore away the B-24s No. 2 engine and left wing with 20mm shells. The plane went into a steep bank and then splashed into Makassar Strait. American crewmen on other planes saw only one chute open before the plane crashed.

Lt. Commander Fujita and two wingmen attacked A/C 568, piloted by Lt. Hal Kendall. The Japanese fighter pilots knocked out the B-24s No. 3 and No. 4 engines. The plane fell off to the left before three more Zeros assailed the crippled Liberator. Withering fire set the B-24 aflame. Three men bailed out before the bomber exploded in midair. These U.S. airmen parachuted downward as the plane crashed into the water. However, the trio were never heard from again. The Japanese had apparently captured and killed them.

But still the American bombers came on, now meeting heavy anti-aircraft fire that filled the sky with a confetti of ebon flak. The big U.S. bombers bounced from the staccato of exploding AA fire. But despite this new danger and the continued attacks by Japanese army and navy fighter planes, the Americans were resolute. Bombardiers ignored the threat of imminent death to pinpoint the target below through their Norden bomb sights.

"IP in one minute, IP in one minute," Bombardier Wes Brown cried into his intercom.

Seconds later, a glob of AA exploded directly under a Long Ranger B-24 piloted by Lt. Ed Kates, a bomber in the same lead box of B-24s. The explosion tore open the belly of Kates's plane before engulfing the Liberator in a ball of flame. The B-24 fell in a cascade of fire and crashed into Balikpapan town.

Still, at 0945, Lieutenant Brown cried into his intercom. "Bombs away!"

Then ten 250 pounders dropped from the lead 307th Group aircraft. Other Long Ranger aircraft also emptied their bomb bays moments later. Regardless of the Japanese harassment, the Americans bombed effectively. 60% of the 250 pounders fell in the area of the Pandansari refinery. The northeast sector of the plant was shattered. Then eight bombs from the 307th B-24s hit the Edeleanu plant to erupt a series of explosions. More bombs hit a kerosene storage tank that exploded in a ball of fire and smoke. Other bombs struck and destroyed several coolie barracks adjacent to the refinery.

Col. Bob Burnham sighed in relief as he led his B-24s away from target. Despite the heavy interception and AA opposition his group had done quite well in the bombing runs.

The 5th Bomb Group, following the 307th, enjoyed even better success. The group's gunners had dealt with the Japanese fighter pilots with more luck than did the 307th Group. However, perhaps the enemy airmen were somewhat spent by the time the 5th arrived for their bomb run. The Bomber Baron gunners knocked six Zeros out of the sky as the Liberators approached target.

At 0947 hours, from his bombardier compartment on Colonel Musgrave's lead B-24, Fred Bonds cried into his intercom. "Bombs away!"

Then, from an altitude of 14,000 feet, a whistling confetti of 250 pound bombs dropped out of the huge bellies of the Bomber Baron aircraft. Four strings of bombs hit the Edeleanu sulfuric acid plant, the main target for the 5th Bomb Group, erupting fires that spread throughout the plant, while palls of black smoke rose skyward to 8,000 feet. More strings of 250 pounders struck an oil drum factory and ignited more balls of fire and curling smoke.

Bombs from the 5th Group Liberators also struck and destroyed oil worker barracks adjacent to the refinery, while other bombs exploded on warehouses and storage buildings along the Balikpapan Bay shoreline. The Bomber Barons even hit a Sugar Charlie (small supply ship) in the harbor and set the vessel afire.

Col. Tom Musgrave felt satisfied as he led his B-24s away from target. He had done considerable damage to the oil complex. But for the American airmen who had already lost five B-24s, the nightmare had just begun. The Japanese now pounced on the departing American planes with horrifying accuracy. As the B-24s turned and headed for home, the pressing Nippon pilots pursued them like hungry hawks after docile pheasants.

"We will attack them as long as possible," Lt. Commander Fujita told his 20th Kokutai pilots. "Attack in pairs! In pairs!"

133

Similarly, Lieutenant Anabuki spoke to his own pilots of the 7th Air Division's 381st Sentai. "We will chase these interlopers to our limit."

Then all across the Makassar Strait, diving Oscars, Tonys, and Zeros made continual passes at the droning B-24s. The Japanese caused more damage to aircraft, killed and wounded more airmen, and downed more B-24s.

One Japanese fighter pilot rammed A/C 101 of the 307th Bomb Group in the right wing after the Liberator's bombing run. The B-24 turned on its back, went down in a dive, and crashed into the sea, killing all aboard.

Japanese pilots also attacked A/C 599 which caught machine gun fire and 20mm hits in the left wing and left engines. The Long Ranger plane began to smoke badly and other B-24s tried to protect the damaged aircraft. But the smoking Liberator took a 180 degree erratic turn and wobbled northeast. Radio messages indicated that some of the crew members were abandoning the plane and crewmen on other planes saw two parachutes floating down a moment later. But then, the B-24 plopped into Makassar Strait, while three Zeros and a Japanese float plane circled low over the downed Liberator.

The 5th Bomb Group also suffered more losses. A/C 0467 took 20mm shell fire hits in the fuselage and the B-24 burst into flames before the Liberator crashed into the strait. Col. Tom Musgrave radioed the plane's position to the American submarine on rescue duty, and he also tried to contact someone aboard the downed aircraft over his VHF D Channel. But the 5th Group commander got no reply. Apparently all aboard were killed.

Another 5th Group plane exploded in midair from severe Japanese shell fire that ripped open the belly of the big bomber which exploded and apparently killed all aboard. The Liberator then fell into Makassar Strait.

The Japanese had shown unusual aggressiveness and accuracy, much better than they had on the 29 September raid. Apparently, the army pilots of the 381st Sentai had been encouraged by the bold, undaunted naval pilots of the 20th Kokutai under Lt. Cmdr. Nobuo Fujita. Lieutenant Anabuki was delighted with the efforts of his pilots, who never faltered in their pressing attack.

Not until the 307th and 5th Bomb Groups had reached the coast of Celebes Island did the Japanese airmen from Balikpapan finally break off the attack. In fact, the Japanese had harassed the American bomber crews in a running battle for an astonishing one hour and fifteen minutes.

And still the Japanese were not finished. As the American planes crossed the Celebes isthmus and droned eastward over the Tomini Gulf, 382nd Sentai fighter planes under Lt. Masayuki Nakase rose out of Manado, while 22nd Kokutai fighter planes under Cmdr. Joyotara Iwami rose again from Kendari. The Japanese air units then zoomed toward the American formations. As the American bomber crews crossed the gulf, they clashed with their Japanese adversaries.

Again, American gunners unleashed heavy .50 caliber machine gun fire, while Japanese pilots loosened 7.7mm wing fire and 20mm cannon fire. American fire tore holes in wings, fuselages, tails, and canopies, killing or wounding Nippon pilots, and damaging or downing Nippon planes. But the Americans too suffered death, injury, and damage from the tormenting Japanese pilots who downed two more American B-24s over the Tomini Gulf and Molucca Sea, while the Japanese lost six fighter planes.

Finally, the tight diamonds of B-24s flew too far eastward and Commander Iwami broke off the attack. He took his 22nd Kokutai back to Kendari, while Lt. Nakase took his 382nd Sentai back to Manado. Fortunately, Japanese planes from Bitjoli in the Halmaheras and from Amboina on Ceram Island failed to find the battered B-24 formations.

At about 1400 hours, after being airborne for 12 hours, the sky finally grew quiet, with only the roar of B-24 engines breaking the silence. Both Burnham and Musgrave spent the next half hour gathering reports on casualties. The 307th Group had lost an astonishing seven B-24s, while four had turned back with serious damage. Burnham had also suffered damage to 11 other planes. Thus, only two of the planes from the Long Ranger group had escaped unscathed. Further, Burnham had lost more than a hundred men killed or wounded.

Col. Musgrave's 5th Group had suffered only slightly less. He had lost four B-24s, while sustaining serious damage to nine more. The Bomber Barons had also suffered over fifty men killed or wounded.

The toll against the Liberator groups had been the highest on any single mission in the Pacific since the B-24 first went into combat in late 1942. Both group commanders hoped they would never again endure such a nightmarish ordeal.

But Musgrave and Burnham were wishfully thinking. No matter what the cost or losses, the American B-24 crews would return to Balikpapan.

Chapter Nine

All during the day of 4 October, 1944, pilots of the 9th Fighter Squadron at Cape Sansapor had been discussing the heavy losses of the B-24 groups during their three missions to Balikpapan. The pilots felt a mixture of sadness and frustration because they had not been able to escort the heavy bombers on these dangerous runs.

In recent weeks, these U.S. fighter pilots had been relegated to mop up and milk run operations in the eastern islands of the Indies and over western New Guinea because the major targets were now in the Philippines and western Pacific, far out of range of American fighter planes. The 9th Squadron P-38s were 936 miles from Balikpapan and the Lightnings could not make this long journey.

Major Wallace Jordan and his 9th Squadron Head-hunters would have enjoyed an escort mission to Balikpapan and the opportunity to engage Japanese fighter pilots. Jordan and his pilots had tasted a good dogfight a few days ago when they had routed the Japanese 19th Kokutai out of Bitjoli on 29 September.

The agony suffered yesterday by the airmen of the 307th and 5th Bomb Groups had preyed on Jordan's mind all day. The 9th Squadron commander was sure that if he and his Headhunters had accompanied the B-24s, the heavy bomber groups would not have endured those heavy losses. For the past 24 hours,

Jordan had mulled in his mind a unique idea, one as daring as it was reckless.

At the evening mess in the 9th Squadron officers mess, the pilots ate their usual fare of bully beef, dehydrated potatoes, canned peas, and canned peaches. As expected, they talked of the B-24 missions over Balikpapan and the Headhunters own inability to help the Liberator airmen. Lt. Ed Howes, a young pilot, looked at his commander.

"Major, are those guys from the 307th and 5th Groups going back to that oil refinery complex?"

"Yes, from what I hear," Jordan answered.

"They'll get mauled again," Howes said. "They got hit hard a few days ago and even worse yesterday. Maybe none of them'll get back next time."

"Eddie's right, Wally," Maj. Dick Bong suddenly spoke. "It's too bad we can't do something."

The other 9th Squadron officers looked at Bong, a man who was already a legend in the SWPA and a household name back in the United States. He had downed more than 30 Japanese planes in combat and on one occasion he had knocked down five planes during a single engagement. In two other instances, he had knocked down four planes in each foray. General Kenney had finally grounded the fearless, adventurous Bong and sent the air ace home.

However, Bong had grown restless and irritated in the States and he had wheedled his way back to the Pacific. But Kenney had insisted that Bong had seen enough combat and he had confined him to limited flying—patrols and recon sorties; no combat. Bong had come to his advanced U.S. fighter base at Cape Sansapor presumably to offer advice and suggestions to the Headhunter pilots, but he had not yet returned to FEAF headquarters in Hollandia.

General Kenney did not press for the major's recall, confident that the Army Air Force's favorite son could not get into much trouble at Sansapor. Enemy fighter pilots were practically non-existent in western New Guinea and the eastern areas of the Indies where the 9th Squadron had been recently flying its missions. After Bong spoke at the mess table, Capt. Harry Brown leaned from his chair.

"You're supposed to be here in Sansapor to advise us, Major," Brown said to Bong. "Do you have any suggestions?"

"I wish I did," Bong answered, shaking his head.

Maj. Wallace Jordan had been listening to the chit chat in silence. But then the 9th Squadron commander took a long swig of his coffee, set the cup down carefully, and then spoke, "Gentlemen, there is a way. There's a way we can escort those B-24s the next time they go out to hit that oil complex."

"Major," Captain Brown grinned, "there's no way we can fly nine hundred and thirty six miles. Even Morotai is eight hundred and forty five miles to Balikpapan and we couldn't make Borneo even if we staged from there."

"We can make Borneo and come halfway back with auxiliary gas tanks," Jordan said. "We could make it to the Molucca Sea or maybe even as far east as the Djailalo Passage."

"Then what?" Bong grinned. "Do we swim the rest of the way back to Sansapor?"

"Something like that," Jordan answered. "We could ditch in the Molucca Sea at a pre-determined point where a submarine or PBYs could pick us up. Belly tanks would enable us to reach Makassar Strait. We'd have enough gas in our regular tanks to have a good donnybrook over Balikpapan with any Nip fighters and then fly back as far as the Halmaheras."

"Major, you've got to be kidding," Captain Brown said.

But Wallace Jordan did not answer.

Now, the faces about the mess table suddenly sobered. They looked intently at their 9th Squadron commander for they realized that Jordan was not kidding. Then, Dick Bong leaned forward and grinned again. "Goddamn, Wally, do you think we could really do that?"

"Dick," Jordan said, "everyone of us knows our infantry guys are going into Leyte in two or three weeks: One hundred thousand guys from a half dozen combat divisions and a half dozen service divisions. Any Nips who reach that American beachhead in a truck or in a tank, inside a plane, or aboard a ship is a potential killer of a GI. Every gallon of gas that doesn't reach the Philippines from Balikpapan may mean that one Nip can't reach Leyte to kill or maim an American dogface. What are we?" he gestured. "Twenty fighter pilots. If we can deal with Nip fighter planes so the B-24s can finish off the Balikpapan refineries, just think how many guys won't catch a Jap bullet or a Jap shell or a Jap bomb in the Philippines. Anyway, I don't think any of us will get lost. If the Catalinas or the subs know our position, they'll pick us up. What the hell are fifteen P-38s compared to those thousands of dogfaces?"

"Not much," Harry Brown said.

"Of course," Jordan gestured, "I wouldn't ask anybody to do this; it would be a strictly volunteer caper."

"Wally," Dick Bong shook his head, "They'll never go for it; not Whitehead, not Kenney, not anybody."

"I'll be flying down to Owi tomorrow and I'll talk to Charlie King of the 35th Fighter Group. If he goes along with this idea, maybe they won't turn down two of us."

"Well sir," Lt. Ed Howes said, "If they okay this thing, I want in."

"I'll remember that, Lieutenant," Jordan said.

"God, that'd be something," Captain Brown said, shaking his head. "We could have a ball. There'll just be a hell of lot more of those bastards flying around Balikpapan than we'll ever find over the Halmaheras."

"That's for sure," Dick Bong nodded.

The next morning, 5 October, Wally Jordan flew to Owi Island off Biak, in the Schouten Islands group and about 150 miles southeast of Sansapor. Based here at the single airfield was the U.S. 35th Fighter Group, a veteran unit in the Pacific that had seen 2½ years of combat and a unit that had nurtured such aces as Majors Tom Lynch, Ken Sparks, Paul Stanch, and most of all Dick Bong himself. Bong had scored most of his 30 kills while flying with the 35th before the American ace returned to the States.

Maj. Charlie King, CO of the 35th's 41st Squadron, had himself already scored a dozen kills and he, like other U.S. fighter pilots, had become bored with his inability to find and engage Japanese fighter pilots. He especially yearned to fight Nippon airmen with the squadron's powerful P-47 fighter plane that Japanese

142

pilots found almost impossible to knock down. But like the pilots of the 9th Squadron, King and his pilots had found little opportunity for dog fights because few Japanese planes were any longer this far east.

When King heard Jordan's suggestion of escorting B-24s to Balikpapan and then ditching in the sea on the way home, King listened in fascination. The very audacity of such a caper appealed to the 41st Squadron commander. King knew that about 200 enemy planes had jumped the B-24s during this most recent mission to Balikpapan. He also knew that the 9th Squadron had enjoyed a delightful time against the enemy fighters out of Bitjoli and the 41st Squadron major would have liked a similar experience.

"It's a hell of an idea, Wally," King said, "but Whitehead will never go for it and neither will FEAF."

"I'd still like to see General Whitehead," Jordan said. "We'd have better chances if I had your support."

"Every guy in my squadron would go, including me," King said, "and so would the guys in the 40th Squadron."

The two squadron leaders then approached the 5th Air Force commander. Ennis Whitehead listened with interest but he then shook his head. "I couldn't let you do that."

"But only volunteers would go," Jordan said.

"I'll be goddamned if we'll dump fifty or sixty fighter planes in the sea," the general barked, "not with the Philippine invasion coming up in about three weeks. We'll need every pilot and plane we can get our hands on. Engineers have just about finished that air-

143

strip on Morotai and the 35th and 49th Fighter Groups will be moving there soon to support the Leyte invasion."

"But FEAF is supposed to knock out those refineries," Jordan persisted. "If the heavies can do that, sir, won't things be a hell of a lot easier in the Philippines for the infantry guys?"

"I'm sorry," Whitehead said. "I can't let you do it. But, I'll take up your suggestion with General Streett and General Kenney."

However, when Whitehead relayed Jordan's idea to Kenney, the FEAF commander responded with a blunt no. He would not jeopardize his fighter planes nor expose their pilots in such an adventure, no matter how many flyers were willing to volunteer. General Streett, despite the heavy losses in the B-24 groups during the first two Balikpapan raids, agreed with Kenney. The 13th Air Force general, the OTC for the Balikpapan air operations, had resigned himself to heavy tolls on the continued B-24 runs to Balikpapan. Even Col. Tom Musgrave and Col. Bob Burnham, whose heavy bomber groups had taken the severe losses, agreed that they could not ask U.S. fighter pilots to fly to Borneo without fuel to return to base. The Bomber Baron and Long Ranger commanders feared that such a tactic would amount to suicide, especially if the P-47s and P-38s became heavily engaged with Japanese fighter pilots.

When the men of the 307th and 5th Groups heard of Jordon's proposal, the bomber crews expressed admiration for these fighter pilots who were willing to fly out to Balikpapan and then ditch. But the air crews also agreed that such tactics would be inappropriate—like going to sea in ships they knew would sink.

During the remainder of early October, another heavy weather front closed in the Netherlands East Indies, with dense rain clouds extending all the way from the Indian Ocean, across Borneo, the Celebes, the Halmaheras, and well into New Guinea. The front hung on for several days, ruling out any new missions to Balikpapan. The respite enabled the Japanese 4th Air Fleet to send replacement aircraft and pilots to their bases in the East Indies. Further, the Japanese worked feverishly and without harassment to repair the refineries which had suffered much more damage on the 3 October raid than they had during the 29 September raid.

Yet, if the Japanese appreciated these days of forced inactivity by the American air forces due to the inclement weather, the delay, ironically, worked against them.

Gen. Clement McMullen had been appointed chief of FEAF Service Command in June of 1944 by General George Kenney. McMullen had been an aircraft maintenance and repair officer since joining the Army Air Force in the 1920s, and he had spent much of his time on the improvement of combat aircraft. He had been responsible for turning fighter planes into fighter-bombers, he had devised the tail gunner compartment on heavy bombers to protect such aircraft from interceptions that came from the rear, and he had introduced the auxiliary gas tank on aircraft that gave such planes more range. Most recently, he had developed the bomb bay gas tanks on B-24s that had

145

enabled these heavy bombers to make the long range missions to Balikpapan.

For many months, both U.S. bombers and U.S. fighters had carried auxiliary gas tanks in the Pacific war, since combat missions often entailed long flights over a wide expanse of ocean. When FEAF first suggested the series of bombing raids to Balikpapan in early September, McMullen had designed the bomb bay tanks for the B-24s so the planes could make this long round trip. He also recognized the danger of sending Liberators through 1200 miles of enemy territory without fighter escorts. So McMullen had immediately put his engineers to work in devising some means of increasing the range of P-38s and P-47s so they could make a long round trip to Balikpapan. The task was formidable since a round trip to Borneo would be the longest flight ever made by fighter planes during World War II.

However, McMullen and his aviation engineers proved equal to the task.

The general and his technicians had come up with a unique idea. Instead of using the standard 375 gallon auxiliary fuel tank on the fighter plane, they would install two tanks, one of 310 gallons under the right wing and another of 165 gallons under the left wing. The pilot could drop the bigger tank as he approached the combat zone, while the smaller 165 gallon tank would be no problem for the fighter plane if the P-47 or P-38 pilot engaged in combat. McMullen had tested the technique during the last two weeks of September and on 6 October he met with General Kenney and announced that he could modify the Lightning and Thunderbolt fighter planes so these aircraft could carry enough fuel for a round trip to Balikpapan, including at least a half hour's fuel for combat time.

General Kenney did not doubt McMullen because the FEAF commander knew that his technical chief had never failed. He ordered the tanks installed at once on as many P-47s and P-38s as possible within the next two days. He asked that only volunteers, however, should fly this long mission with the twin auxiliary fuel tanks. McMullen knew that Wally Jordan and Charlie King had offered fighter cover for the B-24s, so the FEAF service chief singled out their units for the dual fuel tank installations.

By the end of the day, 8 October, McMullen could report to Kenney that 60 fighter planes would be available for the next mission to Balikpapan, 18 P-38s of the 9th Fighter Squadron and 42 P-47s of the 35th Fighter Group's 41st and 40th Squadrons.

Both General Kenney and General Streett were delighted and they now decided to go for broke. The next strike on Balikpapan would be the most massive heavy bomber attack ever conducted in the SWPA. Kenney ordered all five B-24 groups of the 13th and 5th Air Forces to participate in the third raid on the Borneo oil complex.

"When can the B-24s get off?" Kenney asked Streett.

"They're ready now," Streett answered, "and meteorologists say the weather should be clearing on the 9th."

"Okay, then plan the FO for the 10th."

"Yes sir," Streett answered.

Streett called a conference at ADVON headquarters in Noemfoor for the morning of 8 October, bringing in the five commanders of the B-24 groups, the commander of the night bombardment squadron, and the two commanders of the fighter plane units. In attendance were Colonel Musgrave of the 5th Group, Colonel Burnham of the 307th Group, Col. Ed Scott of the 90th Group, Col. Jim Potty of the 43rd Group, Col. Richard Robinson of the 22nd Group, and Lt. Col. James Dunkell of the 868th Night Squadron, the radar equipped unit that could operate in the dark. Also here were Major King of the 35th Group, who would lead the unit's 41st and 40th Squadrons, and Major Jordan of the 9th Headhunter Squadron.

"Gentlemen," Streett began, "we've already caused considerable damage to the Balikpapan oil complex, but now we're going all out. We'll be sending out anything that can fly to Borneo. Colonel Murtha and I have drawn up FO 135 and it's a rather complicated field order that will require the closest kind of cooperation. The show will begin on the evening of 9/10 October."

"We'll start with night harassment raids over Balikpapan," Col. John Murtha said. "We plan to send seven B-24s from the 43rd Group's 63rd Squadron over Balikpapan at one hour intervals to keep Japanese pilots awake for most of the night. That way, they won't be too alert for interception attacks in the morning. Then just before the main bombardment formations arrive, the 868th Squadron will drop a thousand pieces of window strips to screw up the enemy's radar. The B-24s will start dropping the windows from sixty miles out of Balikpapan along the entire route into target."

"We'll be going in with our windows at about 0830 hours, is that right?" Lt. Col. John Dunkell of the 868th asked.

"That's fine, Colonel," Murtha answered.

"The P-47 Squadrons will precede the B-24s over Balikpapan," Streett gestured. "They'll come in at about twenty thousand feet to take on Japanese fighter planes which rise off Manggar or Samarinda Fields to intercept. The P-38s from the 9th Squadron will hang close to the B-24s to attack any Japanese interceptors which get through the P-47 units."

"We'll be arriving at Balikpapan at about 1000 hours; is that right, sir?" Major King asked.

"Yes," Murtha answered.

"If the P-47s do well," General Streett said, "they should clear the way for the heavy bombers to plaster the refineries." He pulled down a wall map and then turned to the air commander again. "Here's the Balikpapan oil complex. Some of you are already familiar with it. The 13th Air Force Groups, the 307th and 5th, will come in first. The 307th will devote all efforts to bombing the cracking plant down here at the south end of the complex. The 5th Group will bomb the paraffin-lube oil plant just above the cracking plant. The 90th Group will drop all of its bombs on the Pandansari refinery and on the Edeleanu plant here to the north to complete the destruction of these two areas. The 22nd Group will come in behind the 90th and finish off whatever is left of the main Pandansari plant. The 43rd Group squadrons will come last to complete the destruction of the paraffin plant along with the destruction of the boiler house, water treatment plant, and power station. If all goes well, there should be nothing left but rubble at Balikpapan. It would take the Japanese at least a month to make repairs so they can start piping fuel out of there again. By then, our ground troops would be well entrenched in the Philippines."

"Rendezvous will be over Cape Manimbaja, as usual," Col. Murtha said.

"Colonel," Major King suddenly spoke, "our fighters will be carrying their twin auxiliary fuel tanks and we won't drop the larger ones until we reach the target area. What happens if the Japanese send out fighter interceptors from their bases in the Halmaheras and Celebes? They gave the heavies an awful rough time the other day."

"We're leaving that problem to the 8th Fighter Group and the other squadrons of the 49th Fighter Group," Murtha said. "These squadrons of P-47s and P-38s will carry the standard three hundred and seventy-five gallon auxiliary tanks and escort the B-24s as far as the Celebes. They'll intercept any Japanese planes that come out of Bitjoli, Amboina, Manado, or Kendari. The squadrons with the twin tanks will not engage if at all possible. Of course," he gestured, "on the way back you won't have the big auxiliary tanks and you'll need to deal with any interceptions out of the Celebes and Halmaheras."

"Yes sir," King answered.

"The 9th, 41st, and 40th Squadrons will accompany the heavy bomb groups all the way to and from target. These squadrons will fly up to Morotai the first thing in the morning," Streett said. "When you take off on the 10th you'll only be eight hundred and forty-five miles from Borneo instead of nine hundred and thirty-six miles. That gives you an extra two hundred miles. The bombers will rendezvous over Cape Manimjaba as Colonel Murtha pointed out and the fighters from Morotai will join them over the Molucca Sea at latitude 126 E by longitude 2.1 south. That means these fighters will skip the Halmaheras altogether but the other fighter units of the 8th and 49th Groups will take on Japanese interceptors from the Halmaheras and Ceram Island."

"Are there any more questions?" Colonel Murtha asked.

"What about weather?" Jordan asked.

"As far as we know, the skies should be clear throughout the East Indies on 10 October," the 13th Air Force operations officer said.

"On this mission, our B-24s will carry five hundred pound bombs," Streett said. "The two hundred and fifty pounders were okay to start fires and to fracture plants, but now we want to flatten the entire complex. Unfortunately, because of heavy fuel loads, each plane can only carry five of these five hundred pounders."

"Any other questions?" Murtha asked.

None.

"Okay, get back to your units," Streett said. "Have your squadron and flight leaders read the FO carefully when you meet with them and your crews for briefings. Make certain that each flight, each plane, and each man knows exactly what his job will be. He must carry out his role with no mistakes."

On the morning of 9 October, Major Charles King led 42 P-47s of the 49th Group's 41st and 40th Squadrons to Morotai from their base at Owi.

Similarly, Maj. Wally Jordan led 18 P-38s of the 9th Squadron out of Cape Sansapor to Morotai. Among the pilots in the flight was Major Dick Bong, who had convinced Jordan to take him on the mission. The noted air ace would be halfway to Balikpapan before an angry General Kenney learned that Bong had gone off on this dangerous mission. Finally, P-38s and P-47s of the 8th Fighter Group and 49th Fighter Group flew to Cape Sansapor to fly out on escort as far as the Celebes.

All total, 136 big bombers and 96 fighters would participate in the 10 October 1944 raid on the important Japanese oil complex.

At twilight, 9 October, seven B-24 snoopers of the 43rd Bomb Group, staging out of Noemfoor, began taking off for the long flight to Balikpapan. The Liberators from the Ken's Men group would leave here at one hour intervals on solo flights to harass the Japanese all night from midnight to 0700. Ken's Men B-24s would orbit over Balikpapan for an hour and then drop their confetti of 100 pound bombs indiscriminately, thereby rendering all Japanese housing areas unsafe.

Also on 9 October, 22 B-24s of the 90th Group, 20 from the 22nd Group, and 20 from the 43rd Group arrived at Noemfoor to stage for the Balikpapan mission. Ground and service crews had never seen so many Liberators in one place. The big bombers had seemingly taken up every square yard of space on this Geelvink Bay airbase. Personnel found themselves unusually pressed to care for the horde of airmen visitors: housing them, feeding them, and giving them comfort before the long flight to Balikpapan.

Shortly after midnight, 10 October, eight B-24s from the radar equipped 868th Night Bomb Squadron took off from Noemfoor. They would be over the target area by 0830 to drop their window metal stripping for disrupting the Japanese radar screens.

At 0200 hours, Tom Musgrave roared down the Kornaseron runway at Noemfoor the first of 121 B-24s loaded with 500 pound demo and incendiary bombs. Behind Musgrave came Lieutenant Russell, Lieutenant Gutheil, Maj. James Pierce, and 20 more Liberators of the Bomber Barons. Immediately behind the 5th, Bob Burnham roared down the runway in his lead B-24 of the 307th Group. Following him came Lieutenant Covington, Lieutenant Forke, Major Reese, and 21 more Long Ranger planes.

By 0300 hours, after the 13th Air Force groups took off, the three groups from the 5th Air Force left Noemfoor. First down the runway were the 22 B-24s of the 90th Group. Behind the Jolly Rogers came 18 B-24s of the 22nd Bomb Group, and finally 19 Liberators of the 43rd Group followed the Red Raiders.

At Cape Sansapor, 36 P-38s from the 49th and 8th Fighter Groups began taking off at 0500 hours. These planes would meet the B-24 formations off the northwest coast of New Guinea and escort the bombers beyond the Halmaheras and over the Celebes. The Lightning pilots would take on any Japanese interceptors before they returned to Sansapor.

At Morotai, where Army Air Force engineers had recently completed two runways and some 50 revetment areas, ground personnel on the small island had serviced the 16 P-38s of the 9th Squadron and 42 P-47s of the 41st and 40th Squadrons. At 0530 hours,

Charlie King roared down the runway in his lead fighter plane. Within a half hour, 41 more Thunderbolts took off. The P-47s would fly westward with their twin auxiliary tanks to meet the B-24s over the Molucca Sea. Right behind the P-47s, Wally Jordan zoomed from Morotai airstrip in the lead P-38 of his 9th Squadron. Following him were 17 more fighter pilots before the P-38s jelled into formation and followed the P-47s southwestward. These Lightnings would also join the B-24s over the Molucca Sea beyond the Halmaheras.

By 0600 hours, the American air bases had become dormant. Now ground crews at Morotai, Cape Sansapor, and Noemfoor could only wait and pray. They hoped this massive raid today would finish off once and for all the Balikpapan oil complex, because they did not want to see their combat crews fly out this far again.

Chapter Ten

After an hour in the air, the long formation of American bombers reached Djailalo Passage. Then the U.S. airmen ran into dense clouds. Nose gunner Harold Trout aboard Bob Burnham's lead 5th Group plane squinted at the thick overcast and silently cursed the meteorologists who had promised that the entire route to Borneo would be clear. In the depths of the night, the young gunner did not even see the formation of P-38s from the 8th and 49th Groups that had joined the B-24s. Only when he heard the talk over the VHF channel did he realize that the fighter escorts had arrived.

"This is Blackbird Leader; Blackbird Leader," Col. George Walker of the 49th Group called into his radio.

"We read you, Blackbird," Col. Tom Musgrave answered.

"We'll hang with you as far as the Celebes," Walker said.

"We appreciate that," the 5th Group commander said.

As the planes droned on, the B-24 crews checked their watches or studied the intricate tables that FEAF had set up for the long range mission. Every hour, one waist gunner moved from mid-fuselage to the tail section, and every two hours two crewmen moved up to the flight deck while the co-pilot switched the fuel use from one of the bomb bay tanks to the other auxiliary fuel tank. These measures had been adopted on the long flight to Balikpapan to save fuel. Normally, the B-24 used about 200 gallons of gas per hour, but with these special crew movements and alternating gas usage, the B-24 could save nearly enough gas to earn themselves at least another hour of flying time.

As the FEAF planes crossed the east coast of the Halmaheras, the gunners in the formation alerted themselves for enemy interceptors out of Bitjoli or from Amboina down in Ceram Island. However, because of the dense cloud cover and the darkness, the Japanese could not intercept the American formation. Once again, Lt. Commander Tanaka at Bitjoli could only notify the fighter bases in the Celebes and in Balikpapan that American bombers were again apparently on the way to Borneo. Tanaka was disappointed for he wanted a chance to attack these FEAF bombers. But fate had favored him. Had he taken off, the 19th Kokutai commander would have run into a whirlwind of opposition from American fighter pilots.

Although no Japanese interceptors met the U.S. formation over the Halmaheras, poor weather caused serious confusion. The 5th Air Force Groups had been flying behind the two 13th Air Force Groups at an altitude of 12,500 feet compared to the 5th and 7th Groups who were flying at 8,200 feet. At the lower altitude, Musgrave and his 13th Air Force units slowed down instinctively and continued on instruments. However, the dense overcast and heavy humidity affected the direction compasses so that the 5th and

307th Bomb Groups flew slightly off course to the northwest.

As a result, the 90th, 22nd, and 43rd Groups of the 5th Air Force, flying straight westward at the standard 160 MPH speed, overtook the 13th Air Force Groups. By the time the FEAF formations had cleared the Halmaheras and come over the Molucca Sea, the 5th Air Force groups were some distance ahead of the 13th Air Force groups.

About 100 miles west of the Halmaheras, daylight emerged from the east and Tom Musgrave realized that he was too far north. He called his navigator. "Where the hell are we?"

"At about 0.5 degrees south by 127.1 degrees east."

"Jesus," Musgrave huffed, "we're about a degree off course. Please readjust and get us back on the right flight path."

"Yes sir."

Then, Musgrave noticed something else. None of the fighter planes from the 8th or 49th Groups was anywhere near his formation so far as he could tell.

"What's going on? Where's the escort?"

"I don't know, sir," the co-pilot answered. "That heavy cloud cover apparently threw us off course because magnetic interception and dense humidity hurt our compasses."

Musgrave then called his squadron commanders as well as Bob Burnham of the 307th Group. "Ranger Leader, this is Zorina Leader. We went off course and we're behind schedule and out of position. We lost both the 5th Air Force heavy groups and the fighter cover."

"Goddamn," Burnham answered. Then, a few

minutes later, he called Musgrave. "I checked with my own crews. None of them has seen Bison units behind us or Blackbird units around us. We must have become separated as we came over the Halmaheras. They may be ahead of us; maybe they apparently passed us while we flew through those clouds banks and got slightly off course."

"Maybe," Musgrave said.

"What do you suggest?" the 307th Group commander asked.

"We'll just keep on going," Musgrave said. "I don't think we should break radio silence to contact Bison until we get within radio range of target, or unless we're sure the Japanese know where we are."

"Okay, Colonel," Burnham said.

The disappearance of both the fellow B-24 groups and the fighter cover brought an uneasiness to the 5th and 307th Groups airmen. The Bomber Barons and Long Rangers feared they might once again find themselves fighting off alone a horde of aggressive Japanese pilots.

Gunners Jim Shaw, Merv Anderson, and Harold Trout aboard the lead 5th Group Liberator held the triggers of their guns a little tighter as the sky grew brighter from the emerging daylight and suddenly clearing skies. Aboard Jim Russell's plane, gunners Joe Tribble, Charlie Smith, and Hal Phillips scanned the skies vigorously for any sign of Japanese fighter planes. In Lt. Ken Gutheil's *Blackjack*, Gunners Chuck Lee and Wes Barker studied with uneasiness the clearing weather: a blue sky above them and a full view of the Molucca Sea below them.

In the 307th Group, Gunners Sam Leffort and Ed

Anderson also felt apprehension as they peered nervously from their waist and nose gun positions respectively. On Lt. Ron Covington's plane, Sgt. Joe Black once more checked the armor belts for his .50 caliber gun. Black had already downed two Japanese planes on the first two raids, but he was not anxious to get another opportunity against enemy fighters because he might become a victim this time instead of a victor. Aboard A/C 570, Sgt. Ralph O'Brien jerked when Lt. Don Forke spoke over the intercom.

"Stay alert! Stay alert! We lost Bison and our Blackbird cover. We don't know what's up ahead."

"Yes sir," O'Brien answered.

And indeed, the Bomber Barons and Long Rangers had reason to worry. Below them, on the relatively calm Molucca Sea, Capt. Zenji Orita had been sailing on just the right latitude in his north-south axis to detect the American bombers. His lookout men aboard submarine I-176 got a close look at the 13th Air Force bombers, while Orita's radar men got clear blips on their screens.

"Enemy bombers flying westward at eight thousand feet," the lookout told Orita.

"Enemy formation on a course of 178 degrees, true, almost due west," the radar officer said. "They fly at approximately eight thousand two hundred feet at about three hundred kilometer per hour speed. They can be expected to reach the east coast of the Celebes in about an hour."

"How many bombers are there?"

"About fifty, Honorable Commander," the radar officer said.

"And, of course, they have no escort?"

"No, Captain, it does not appear so."

"No," Orita nodded, almost to himself. "They could not bring fighter planes with them on such a long flight from New Guinea to Balikpapan, their obvious destination today as it was twice before. You will notify the air commanders at Manado and Kendari that American bombers are once more flying westward," Orita told his radio operation. "The enemy formation will cross the Celebes coastline in about an hour."

"Yes, Captain."

Within moments, the radar reports from Submarine I-176 reached both Kendari and Manado. The OD's immediately relayed the information to the fighter unit commanders.

At Kendari, Captain Sonokawa was already awake. The 23rd Air Flotilla commander, who maintained his flotilla headquarters here, usually awoke about dawn and sat down to a leisurely breakfast before the burst of morning activity at this major Japanese airbase. A messenger from his headquarters quickly found the 23rd Flotilla commander to report the flight of the American bombers.

"So," Sonokawa mused, "they have decided to come again. I assume that Commander Iwami has also been given this report?"

"Yes, Honorable Captain."

"And has Commander Iwami called his pilots to an immediate briefing?"

"I believe so."

"You will call at once the headquarters of the Makassar Base Force to report this enemy formation."

He paused and then queried; "How many bombers are there?"

"Perhaps fifty."

"And, of course, they have no escorts?"

"It does not appear that fighter aircraft accompany them."

Sonokawa squinted upwards and then commented; "They suffered badly on their last attack against the refineries. Today, in these clear skies, they will suffer even more. Do your duty," he told the messenger. "I will attend Commander Iwami's briefing myself."

"Yes, Captain."

Cmdr. Joyotara Iwami, meanwhile, had kept his fighter planes and pilots of the 22nd Kokutai on continual alert since the 3 October American attack. As the days passed without new U.S. air formations passing over the Celebes, the personnel of the 22nd had begun to grumble. Perhaps the Americans would not come back after their near disaster on the last bombing mission. But, Iwami had been adamant and now, his patient vigilance had seemingly paid off.

Captain Sonokawa had only spoken briefly with Commander Iwami, reminding the 22nd Kokutai commander to urge his men to full effort against the Americans. The 23rd Flotilla commander had faith in Iwami and he knew his subordinate would act reasonably when Iwami met with his pilots. Captain Sonokawa would merely sit as a spectator and listen. He did not wish to undermine Iwami and give the fighter pilot an impression that he did not trust the judgment of the 22nd Kokutai leader, or that Iwami was not in command.

"We will mount thirty-two aircraft," Iwami said.

161

"Ensign Ishihara will lead the Kawasaki (Tony) aircraft and I myself will lead the Nakajima (Oscar) flights."

"I understand," Lt. Susumu Ishihara answered.

"We will attack from nine and six o'clock in our usual double aircraft passes," Iwami continued. "Each pair of aircraft will come in immediately behind the preceding one. Aircraft will attack in four plane units against each enemy bomber. Do the best you can to destroy the enemy bombers which carry the squadron and flight leaders for the bombardiers as such B-24s will direct the bombing strikes."

"We will do so," Ensign Ishihara answered.

"As soon as the enemy bombers are within radar range and we know exactly where they are, we will take off." He turned to a radar man. "Stay alert at your position. The reports from the submarine indicate the enemy should come within range in about an hour."

"Yes, Honorable Commander."

When the briefing ended, Captain Sonokawa spoke to his pilots. "Be sure you follow Commander Iwami's suggestions without fail. Meanwhile, we have notified the base commander at Balikpapan that these enemy bombers are on the way. Remember," he gestured, "the more of these Yankee aircraft we can destroy or damage, the easier will be the task for the defenders of the Balikpapan refineries."

To the north, in the Celebes base of Manado, Lt. Masauyki Nakase had also responded quickly to the radar reports from I-176. The 382nd Sentai commander had also kept his fighter planes and pilots on continual alert. Like the pilots of the 22nd Kokutai, these airmen too had complained when they had seen no new American bomber formations heading for Borneo during the past week. They too believed that the Americans had given up further attempts to bomb the oil refineries after the heavy losses of October 3. However, like Iwami, Lt. Nakase had nonetheless insisted that his airmen remain on alert.

Now the 382nd Sentai commander called his pilots to a quick briefing. "I am told that our navy pilots at Kendari will attack the enemy bombers from the south. We shall attack these Yankee interlopers from the north. Flight Officer Hiromichi will lead the flights of Nakajima (Oscar) fighters and I will lead the flights of Mitsubishis (Zeros).

"Will there be coordination with the navy pilots?" Hiromichi asked.

"I have already contacted Commander Iwami," Nakase answered. "We have planned our attack patterns. The navy aircraft will attack from six o'clock and nine o'clock and we shall attack from three o'clock and from twelve o'clock. They will attack high and we will attack low."

"When will we mount our aircraft?"

"As soon as the enemy bombers come into range."

Thus the Japanese on the Celebes prepared themselves to meet the American bombers. However, both Commander Iwami and Lieutenant Nakase would be in for a shock.

The radar and visual sightings of the American bombers by the men aboard I-176 carried an ironic twist. The sailors had completely missed the 5th Air Force heavy bomb groups and the escorting American fighter planes which had passed the 13th Air Force planes during the confusion of darkness and heavy clouds. The Nippon submarines had only detected the trailing 5th and 307th Bomb Groups' unescorted B-24s. So the Japanese pilots out of Kendari and Manado expected to meet only 50 American bombers in the skies over the Celebes.

But almost a half hour ahead of the 5th and 307th Bomb Groups, the B-24s of the 90th, 22nd, and 43rd Groups were droning westward with 38 Lightnings of the 8th and 49th Fighter Groups. Maj. Vern Ekstrand, in the lead B-24 of the 90th Group, expressed surprise when he discovered that the Liberators of the 5th and 307th were no longer in front of him. He turned to his co-pilot, Lt. Ed Cromwell.

"What happened to the other B-24s?"

"I don't know, sir," Cromwell answered. "They must have gotten lost in those clouds over the Halmaheras."

"Goddamn," Ekstrand cursed. He then called Major Briggs of the 90th's trailing 319th Squadron. "Charlie, we've still got our escorts, but we lost the 307th and 5th Groups. They aren't ahead of us anymore."

"What are we going to do?"

"Forget about them and keep going. We've all got our own assigned targets. We'll simply hit them. The 13th Air Force groups can hit their own targets if or when they reach Balikpapan."

"Okay," Briggs answered.

Ekstrand then called Col. George Walker who was leading the fighters, 14 Lightnings from the 49th's 39th Squadron and 24 P-38s from the 8th Fighter Group. "Colonel," the major said, "we've lost the 13th

Air Force heavies. They got lost somewhere behind us. But we're going on, and we hope the long range fighters rendezvous with us as planned. Meanwhile, keep your pilots on alert. We might engage interceptors out of Manado or Kendari."

"I read you, Major," Walker answered, "but I must tell you, as soon as we reach Tomini Gulf we'll need to turn back."

"I understand," Ekstrand said.

At 0165 hours, blips appeared on the screens at Manado, indicating that aircraft were approaching Tomini Gulf. The operators were astonished. How could these American bombers come into range so soon? Judging by the reports from submarine I-176, these U.S. planes were supposed to be an hour away. The Japanese, of course, had not realized that the forward 5th Air Force units had come into range and not the trailing 13th Air Force Liberator groups which had been detected by the sailors of I-176. Nonetheless, both Lieutenant Nakase and Commander Iwami took off quickly with their fighter pilots.

At about 0700 hours, as the Americans came within three hours of target, the 382nd Japanese Sentai approached the Americans from the north. Lt. Masauyki Nakase could see the small shapes of U.S. planes ahead of him and his eyes widened in surprise. U.S. fighter planes were apparently hanging about the big bombers. He quickly called F/O Tori Hiromichi.

"Do my eyes deceive me? Do these Yankee bombers have escorts with them?"

"I too am shocked, Lieutenant," Hiromichi answered, "for I also can see the escort aircraft. How can these Yankee fighter planes possibly reach Borneo and return to their New Guinea bases, or even to Morotai?"

"This is strange indeed," Nakase said.

"Perhaps they will only come as far as Tomini Gulf and then return to their bases," Hiromichi said. "Should we delay our attack?"

"No," the 382nd Sentai commander answered. "We will attack the American fighter planes as well as their bombers. Commander Iwami will arrive over Tomini Gulf from Kendari with his navy fighter pilots in about a half hour. Meanwhile, we shall begin our attack. I will take the first flight and attack the enemy bombers from twelve and three o'clock and fly off high. The second flight will attack from underneath at twelve and three o'clock and fly off low. Thus, our flights will not run into each other."

"Yes, Lieutenant," Hiromichi answered.

However, Col. George Walker, leading the U.S. fighters, spotted the Japanese planes forming to the north and he called his pilots.

"This is Blackbird Leader, Blackbird Leader. Blackbirds I and II will hit these enemy interceptors. Blackbird III will maintain cover position to the south in case more interceptors come from Kendari."

"Okay, Colonel," the 8th Fighter Group commander answered.

The gunners aboard the B-24s watched the two squadrons of P-38s zoom north, while the other squadron of Lightnings hung close to the bombers.

"Keep formation tight; keep it tight," Maj. Vern Ekstrand cried over the VHF channel. "Gunners stay alert; stay alert for bandits."

The Liberator gunners then tightened their grips on

166

their weapons, waiting to meet any Japanese interceptors that broke through the American fighter screen.

But the American bomber gunners would find little need to use their guns over Tomini Gulf. Nakase had come south with 30 Oscars and Tonys to clash with 24 Lightnings. However, during the past year, the Americans had produced better trained pilots, while the Japanese had lost most of their experienced pilots and were now sending hastily trained airmen into combat. Further, the P-38s and P-47s were far superior to any type of fighter plane the Japanese could amount against the Americans. As the Lightnings approached the Tonys and Oscars of the Japanese 22nd Sentai, Colonel Walker warned his pilots.

"No fancy stuff. Don't play games with them. Use your superiority in speed, climb, and dive to best advantage. Our P-38s can't begin to maneuver like those Nip planes. And remember, these babies we're flying can take plenty of punishment."

So, as mere spectators, the crews aboard the droning B-24s watched the ensuing dogfight to the north. During the short engagement, the American bomber crews found reason to smile. They saw one after another of the Japanese Oscars and Tonys tumble out of the sky, falling into the sea in fragments, or with trailing smoke, or with streaking sheets of flame. The American fighter pilots were mauling the enemy interceptors.

The P-38 pilots had waded into the Japanese 22nd Sentai with heavy strafing fire from eight forward guns. Working in pairs, the Lightning pilots zoomed down on one enemy plane after another, ripping the Japanese formations to shreds. Within five minutes, Nakase had lost ten planes and suffered damage to at least eleven more. He could not continue the one sided contest and he called off the fight.

"There are too many of them, too many," the 382nd Sentai commander cried into his radio. "We will break off and return to base."

"Yes, Honorable Commander," F/O Tori Hiromichi answered.

Foolishly, Nakase had thus abandoned his interception instead of waiting for the navy planes coming from the south. Further, the American fighter planes might have had to break off soon and return to New Guinea because they had reached the extent of their range. Thus, when Commander Iwami finally arrived to attack the Americans, the 22nd Sentai aircraft were gone and Iwami needed to take on three American P-38 Squadrons that still had time to do some fighting before they were forced to return to base. Nonetheless, Iwami pressed his attacks against the U.S. planes. But he suffered the same harsh results as had Lieutenant Nakase.

"Bandits coming in from the south," an 8th Group squadron leader cried into his radio.

"Okay, we'll come back to help out," Colonel George Walker answered.

Moments later, 24 American planes (for the Japanese of the 22nd Sentai had failed to down a single U.S. plane) joined the fourteen P-38s on the port side of the bombers to attack the 30 oncoming Oscars and Zeros out of Kendari.

168

The Lightning pilots, again in pairs, zoomed down on the Oscars and Tonys of the Japanese navy Kokutai with heavy strafing fire and whooshing 37mm cannon fire. The Japanese occasionally sent streams of 7.7 machine gun fire into the American planes, but the tough Lightnings took the hits in stride to frustrate the 22nd Kokutai pilots. In turn, the U.S. airmen blew out of the air one enemy plane after another. Iwami soon lost nine planes, with severe damage to six more. A few Oscars did run the American gauntlet to reach the B-24s, but heavy fire from the Liberator gunners shot down two of them, while the Japanese failed to down any B-24s or even seriously damage any of the big bombers.

Six minutes after the battle began, Cmdr. Joyotara Iwami, the 22nd Kokutai commander, cursed in aggravation. He was forced to call off the interception and return to Kendari in utter defeat. Iwami grumbled as he flew homeward. He got mauled again, as he had been mauled during the Battle of the Philippines Sea over four months ago. These U.S. Army Air Force pilots and their fighter planes had proven themselves as formidable as had the U.S. Navy pilots and aircraft during the ill fated carrier battle last June. Iwami could only hope that the Japanese pilots at Balikpapan were more successful against these Americans.

When the skies were cleared of Japanese planes, Col. Charles Walker called Vern Ekstrand. "We've reached our range limit, Major, and we'll have to turn back. I don't know where the hell the other fighter planes are, but if we don't get out of here, we'll all be ditching in Djailalo Passage."

169

"Okay," Ekstrand answered. "Thanks for your help."

The American fighter planes had barely disappeared to the east and the 90th Bomb Group was just crossing the western neck of the Celebes beyond Tomini Gulf when Gunner Steve Novak, aboard the Major Briggs' *Phyliss J. of Worchester*, cried excitedly into his intercom.

"Major, I think there's more bandits coming in behind us."

"More bandits?"

"Yes sir."

However, before Briggs reacted, a radio call reached the 90th Group formation from the approaching planes. "This is Thirsty Leader; Thirsty Leader," the voice of Maj. Charlie King came over the radio.

"Thirsty!" Ekstrand cried with elation, "Goddamn, you got here. This is Bison Leader. Do you know anything about Zorina and Ranger?"

"Yes sir," King answered. "They're about a half hour behind you and coming on fast. We met them over Check Point 3. The Headhunters are hanging with them and we came on ahead. Zorina and Ranger are making up ground and they should be right behind you by the time you reach IP. We're going on with our Thirsty aircraft to clear the way ahead. Maybe you won't meet too many Zekes by the time you get there."

"Roger, Thirsty," Maj. Vern Ekstrand said. "Good luck."

The men aboard the Liberators of the 90th, 22nd, and 43rd Groups watched the 40 P-47s of the 35th

Group's 41st and 40th Squadrons zoom over them and head across Makassar Strait. The airmen felt a measure of relief. They had seen what other American fighter pilots had done against enemy fighter planes and they hoped that these P-47s scooting beyond them would do the same thing to any Japanese interceptors over Balikpapan.

Meanwhile, the 5th and 307th Bomb Groups, now only 20 minutes behind the 5th Air Force units, were also approaching Makassar Strait. Col. Tom Musgrave called Vern Ekstrand. "Major, don't wait for us. You may as well take the Bison heavies in first and hit your assigned targets. The other groups may as well do the same thing. We'll come in behind you and hit our own targets later."

"Okay," Ekstrand answered.

Musgrave then looked at the ring of P-38s around him—the fifteen Lightnings of the 9th Headhunter Squadron. He felt quite relaxed with this escort at his side. He might have been fully at ease had he known of the recent donnybrook above Tomini Gulf where other U.S. fighter pilots had just ripped apart both a Japanese army and a navy air unit.

At 0900 hours, the radar men at Balikpapan picked up blips on the screens and they quickly called General Ichabangese. "Honorable Commander, enemy aircraft are again approaching Balikpapan."

"They have given us no rest on this regretful day," Ichabangese scowled. "First they harassed us all night, then they jammed our radar, and now they come to bomb us again."

"They are not bombers, General."

"What do you mean, not bombers?"

"The blips are small, more on the order of fighter planes," the radar operator said. "Yes, they are fighter planes."

"Fighter planes!" Ichabangese gasped. "That is impossible. How could their fighter planes come this far from New Guinea? How?" Then he sighed. "But, whatever they are, these aircraft intend to harm us. You will notify Lieutenant Anabuki, Lt. Commander Fujita, and Major Magari at once to prepare to stop these interlopers."

"Yes, Honorable Commander," the radar man said.

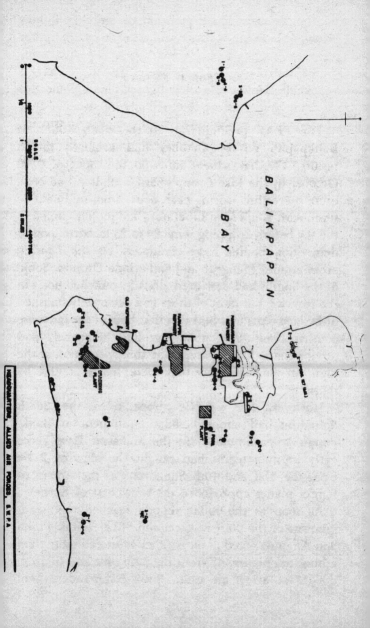

BALIKPAPAN

BAY

Chapter Eleven

The FEAF preliminaries to the main attack at Balikpapan on 10 October had achieved mixed results. The harassment raids on the night of 9/10 October by the 43rd Group's 63rd Squadron had been quite successful. During each hour, from midnight to seven AM, Ken's Men Liberators had merely circled in the sky before dropping some 20 to 25 hundred pound demolition bombs indescriminately on the housing areas around Manggar and Samarinda Dromes. Some of the bombs had destroyed aircraft, punched holes in the runway, but most of them had accurately smashed or burned tents and barracks that housed the Japanese combat flyers, AA troops, ground personnel, and service crews. The Japanese had thus spent most of the night in foxholes and they were hardly rested by morning.

However, the window drops from the 868th Squadron had jammed radar equipment at Balikpapan only minimally, so the Makassar Base Force early warning teams had caught the blips of P-47s from the 41st and 40th Squadrons as the American fighter planes approached the west coast of Borneo.

As soon as the radar reports reached the headquarters of the 20th Kokutai and 381st Sentai, Fujita and Anabuki acted at once. They mustered more than a hundred planes, 42 from the 20th unit and 61 from the 381st army air unit. Both commanders held briefings, while ground crews quickly filled in the 100 pound bomb holes at the Manggar and Samarinda airfields.

"We have a strange report," Lt. Cmdr. Nobuo Fujita told his pilots. "The radar operators insist that the approaching enemy aircraft are fighter planes. I find it impossible to believe that the enemy can send his fighters this far westward. Our first suspicion was that the aircraft came from American carriers that sailed in Makassar Strait, but we have absolutely no evidence that such a naval task force is in the area."

"How many of these fighters are there. Honorable Commander?"

"We have no idea," Fujita answered. "But we must deal with them as we must deal with the Yankee bombers that no doubt are right behind them." He paused and then continued. "I know the enemy's harassment raids last night deprived you of rest, but we must still do our duty. I have already spoken to Lieutenant Anabuki. Our Kokutai will attack these enemy aircraft coming in now and the 381st Sentai will attack the enemy bombers that obviously follow in the wake of these fighter planes."

"Yes, Commander."

"Any questions?" When no one answered, Fujita gestured. "Then let us man our aircraft to stop these Yankee intruders."

At the Manggar Field briefing house, Lt. Satoshi Anabuki also briefed his pilots. "Do not ask how enemy fighter planes can reach Borneo from New Guinea, or even if such reports are accurate. Suffice it to say that the enemy has again come to Balikpapan. Whatever the composition of this first formation of

Yankee aircraft, fighters or bombers, the 20th Kokutai will engage them. The 381st Sentai will attack the American heavy bombers that are surely following."

"Has our radar detected a second formation?" F/O Kuroe asked.

"Not yet, but we can guess that such heavy bombers are on the way," Anabuki answered. "We will make our runs in the usual single column, with each three plane flight attacking one of the enemy bombers."

Then an aide suddenly entered the briefing house and handed Anabuki a report. The 381st Sentai commander read the sheet, scowled, and then looked at his pilots. "This report confirms our suspicions. The enemy's heavy bombers are coming in behind their fighters. Remember, one three aircraft flight to each bomber."

By 0955 hours, Japanese fighter pilots were zooming down the Balikpapan runways to meet the American planes. As soon as Maj. Charlie King saw the dots in the distance, he called his fellow American fighter pilots.

"Bandits up ahead! Bandits! We'll knock out as many as we can."

"Holy Christ, Major," Lt. Bob Johnson gawked, "there's a whole sky full of them out there and we've only got forty planes."

"It doesn't matter, Lieutenant," King said. "We've got to break them up so the heavies can bomb without interception. Drop your three hundred and fifteen gallon tanks and let's go."

"Yes sir," Johnson answered.

The Thunderbolt pilots released their bigger

auxiliary tanks before the P-47s waded toward the Japanese. King called Capt. John Young, the 40th Squadron leader. "Johnnie, take your squadron to port and take on those Nip planes to the left. We'll hit the enemy aircraft to the right."

"Roger, Major," Young answered.

Young would take on the 20th Kokutai with his 40th Squadron, while King took on the 381st Sentai army pilots with the 41st Squadron.

On the ground below, General Ichabangese and chief of staff Koichi Kichi stood on the porch of the general's elaborate Makassar Base Force headquarters and watched the sky full of fighter planes heading toward each other. About the airbase, Japanese ground and service personnel also looked into the clear sky to watch the inevitable clash. And finally, Indonesian civilians at Balikpapan stared upward to study the horde of Japanese planes which were heading for the much smaller number of American fighter planes. Surely, in this instance, the Nippon pilots would triumph.

Only moments later, the donnybrook began. The thunder of .50 caliber and 7.7 machine gun fire, and the thump of 20mm and 37mm shells echoed across the sky. But the spectators soon realized the obvious superiority of the American pilots and their aircraft, as Japanese planes began falling out of the sky like dead birds, fiery rockets, or cascades of smoke.

Major Charlie King and his wingman roared down on a trio of Oscars and opened with chattering machine gun fire and whooshing shells. One Oscar caught a hit in the tail section which fell off before the plane dropped like a rock and crashed into the jungles beyond Balikpapan. Another Oscar caught solid hits in the gas tank. The plane blew up before the fragments dropped to earth like smoking pieces of burning paper. The third Japanese pilot tried to arc away, but King unleashed withering machine gun fire that smashed the cockpit and killed the pilot. The Oscar then tumbled downward to crash and explode in a clearing near Samarinda strip.

"Scratch three, Major," the wingman said.

"Stay alert."

A moment later, a Tony tailed King's wingman and unleashed a stream of 7.7 fire that tattooed the fuselage of the P-47. But the sturdily built Thunderbolt took the hits stoutly and the pilot zoomed swiftly away.

"I told you to stay alert."

"Yes sir," the lieutenant answered.

In the same 41st Squadron, Lt. Bob Johnson got two Tonys within a minute. He dove on a trio of Japanese planes and opened with machine gun fire that chopped off the engine of a Tony. The plane then tumbled downward and crashed into some trees. As the other two Tonys arced away in different directions, Johnson tailed one of them. The Tony pilot tried to zoom upward and away, out of range, but the Japanese plane could not avoid the speedier Thunderbolt. Johnson unleashed a half dozen 37mm shells, two of which severed the fuselage. The Japanese plane then fell tail over nose to crash and explode next to a coolie barracks at Manggar Field.

From the same U.S. squadron, Lt. Jim Mugavaro and his wingman zoomed into a trio of planes. Mugavaro got the lead Oscar with two solid 37mm shell hits that ignited the cockpit and killed the pilot before the Japanese plane fell to earth in a ball of fire. The lieutenant's wingman damaged a second Oscar, while Mugavaro went after the third enemy plane. He came into the Oscar from below with chattering .50 caliber fire and tore open the underbelly of the Japanese plane before the aircraft burst into flames, seemingly stopped in mid air, and then plummeted to earth inside a cloud of enveloping smoke.

The U.S. pilots of the 40th Squadron enjoyed similar success. Capt. John Young, leading his Thunderbolts, got three quick kills. Young had taken his flight down from 19,000 to 9,000 feet when he ran into a tight formation of Zeros. The Japanese pilots attempted to scoot away, but they could not outrun the P-47. Young sprayed the entire formation with raking fire from his eight forward machine guns and a storm of 37mm shells from his wing cannons. The heavy fusillade destroyed two of the Zeros. Young literally tore apart one enemy plane, killing the pilot before the aircraft fell like a mass of debris from the collapsing building. Two of Young's 37mm shells caught the second Zero squarely in the cockpit and engine respectively, killing the pilot and wrecking the Zero. The plane dropped from the formation and tumbled to earth.

As the Japanese planes scattered, Young lined a third Zero in his sights and cut off the plane's wings with rattling machine gun fire. The Japanese aircraft cartwheeled and spun to earth where it crashed and exploded.

"My God, Johnnie," Lt. Bill Strand said, "are you

going to knock down the whole Japanese air force by yourself?"

"There's plenty around, Willie," Young answered. "Help yourself."

And Strand did help himself. He and his wingman, Lt. Hilton Kessel, ran into a formation of four Oscars. The flight leader caught the No. 4 plane of the Japanese formation from dead rear and set the Oscar afire before the plane rolled over and the pilot bailed out. Strand watched the Oscar fall to earth before he zoomed upward and then came down on another quartet of Oscars. This time, Strand jumped the leader and shot off the wing of the Japanese plane before the enemy fighter tumbled to earth. Less than a minute later, Strand caught still another Oscar, shooting off the plane's tail. As the Oscar fell, the Japanese pilot bailed out and the U.S. flight leader watched the striken plane and enemy pilot descend to earth.

"I told you there was plenty for everybody," Captain Young told Strand.

"That's for sure, Johnnie," the flight leader answered.

But when Strand looked around for Lt. Hilton Kessel, he could not find his wingman. They had been separated during the engagement. The lieutenant tried to call Kessel on his radio, but he got no response. Strand's companion was never seen again. Actually, Kessel had been killed by F/O Yasihiko Kuroe who had caught the P-47 with thumping 20mm shells, while Kessel himself was downing a Japanese fighter plane. The Thunderbolt had then exploded, obviously killing Kessel instantly before the plane crashed.

Kessel's death was the only American fighter plane loss during the ten to fifteen minute donnybrook. In turn, the U.S. fighter pilots had shot down 16 enemy fighter planes and damaged at least 20 more quite badly. But most of all, the 41st and 40th Squadron airmen had scattered the Japanese air formations over the hills beyond Balikpapan and over the waters of Makassar Strait. So the American fighter pilots had cleared the route for the heavy bombers which were now droning across the east coast of Borneo. The B-24s had then circled 180 degrees and come over Balikpapan Bay to hit the refineries.

Heavy ack ack fire spewed up at the B-24s as Major Vern Ekstrand led his lead Liberator of the 90th Group over target. His bombardier ignored the countless puffs of ack ack and he carefully sighted his target, the Pandansari refinery. Now, of course, the 20 Liberators of the Jolly Roger group (two had turned back with mechanical trouble) could see the target quite clearly. At 1020 hours, the bombardier on Ekstrand's lead plane dropped his pathfinder flare over the Pandansari refinery. Seconds later, he cried into his radio:

"Bombs away!"

Then fifteen 500 pound demolition bombs dropped out of the bellies of Ekstrand's lead Jolly Roger V. The bombs from the three planes whistled downward and landed squarely atop the huge refinery to explode and ignite fires.

"Right on target, Major," Co-pilot Ed Crowell grinned.

181

"Let's hope the rest of us are just as lucky," Ekstrand said.

Seven more B-24s of the 90 Group's 320th Squadron also unleashed demolition bombs atop the Pandansari refinery. The subsequent explosions erupted more fires, knocked down more of the huge building, wrecked piping, machinery, tanks, and other equipment inside. Palls of heavy smoke and hot fires rose skyward.

"Goddamn," Lt. Frank in *Mann's Morons* grinned. "We flattened that target from end to end."

"It sure looks like it," Co-pilot Al Rehm answered.

But as the first Jolly Roger squadron turned from target and started out to sea, a formation of Zeros flew over the 90th Group aircraft and dropped an array of phosophorous bombs. Most of them missed, but two hit A/C 386 some ten miles east of Manggar Drome. The explosions tore off the nose and right wing before the big bomber fell on its side and dropped to earth in a thunderous explosion. All hands were lost.

Then more enemy fighters attacked the departing B-24s, opening with 7.7 machine gun fire. But the enemy pilots failed to down any B-24s or to seriously damage any of the Liberators before Capt. John Young arrived with a flight of P-47s to chase off the Zeros. The Japanese pilots, still smarting from their earlier defeat, were quite reluctant to take on the P-47s again.

Meanwhile, Maj. Charlie Briggs droned over the Edeleanu plant with the other 90th Group B-24s. Briggs' bombardier also ignored the staccato of AA puffs that exploded about the formation as he carefully studied the target through his Norden bomb sight. Then, at 1105 hours, he released a pathfinder flare and cried into his radio.

"Bombs away!"

The 15 demos dropped from the bellies of this first three plane V, hit squarely on target, and erupted fires that flamed a hundred feet upward. Then came the other 90th Group planes from the 319th and 400th Squadrons. These aircraft also hit the plant to erupt more fire and smoke. The bombardment flattened the Edeleanu factory, while heavy, oily smoke poured from the complex, a newly constructed structure that the Japanese had only completed in August of 1944.

But again, as the B-24s from the 319th and 400th Squadrons turned away from target, 25 to 30 interceptors pounced on the Liberators. Briggs' gunners fired furiously at the attacking planes, downing six of them, with Sgt. Steve Novak, aboard the major's plane, knocking one of the Zeros to pieces before the fragments plopped into the sea. However, the swarm of Zeros seriously damaged five of the Jolly Roger Liberators, killing 17 men and wounding eight. Still, before the Japanese planes could attack again, P-47s from the 40th Squadron jumped the Zeros, shooting down two and chasing off the others.

As fires raged throughout the Pandansari and Edeleanu plant works, the Red Raiders of the 22nd Bomb Group roared over the target with their eighteen Liberators. The Raiders unleashed some of their 500 pounders atop the already burning Pandansari plant, but they also hit the electrical house, drum factory, warehouses, and pipelines. 22nd Group observers could see the extent of their damage, despite the heavy smoke cover. The airmen could see the dotted patches of orange fire that told the U.S. flyers they had badly damaged their targets.

In fact, 40 of the Red Raider bombs had made direct hits and eight had scored near misses, for about a 50% accuracy rate. At least one bomb fell into Balikpapan Bay. As the Red Raiders pulled away from target, smoke rose 1,000 feet high from the drum factory, while smoke and fire totally obscured the warehouses and electrical house.

But, as the 22nd Group Liberators droned out to sea, Oscars and Tonys jumped their tight formation. Most of the passes against the Red Raiders came from ten and two o'clock, ending in upward peel offs. 22nd Group gunners, firing furiously at the attacking Japanese planes, caught one Tony that had a phosphorous bomb under its wing. The Tony flipped over on its back after the hit, went straight down, and burst into flames as it hit the ground. Another Zeke caught hits from a tail gunner and the Japanese plane rolled on its back before dropping and crashing into Balikpapan Bay. Red Raider gunners severely damaged at least three other enemy planes. And again, before the aggressive Japanese pilots made another pass at the 43rd Group bombers, American P-47s came into the fray, quickly downing two of the Zekes and once more scattering the rest.

But the 22nd Group took losses. An enemy plane rammed one B-24 and the resulting explosion killed the Japanese pilot and all those aboard the Liberator. Another Red Raider heavy bomber caught an AA burst that shattered the No. 2 engine. The B-24 then wobbled on precariously with trailing smoke. Observers on other planes saw five chutes open from men who abandoned the plane before the Liberator simply disappeared from sight and presumably crashed into the water.

As the air battle raged, with AA still blackening the sky and fighter planes still zooming about in all directions, the Liberators of the 43rd Bomb Group came over Balikpapan Bay. The Ken's Men had not gotten much sleep last night for they had taken off at 0220 hours after a few hours rest. The target for the 43rd was the huge Edeleanu plant, treatment house, power station, and boiler house.

A Nick Japanese reconnaissance plane had accompanied the 43rd all across the Makassar Strait from the Celebes, staying out of range and watching the Ken's Men closely. The Japanese spotter had undoubtedly given Makassar Base Force headquarters an excellent picture of the heading, speed, and altitude of the 43rd Bomb Group planes because AA fire from the Japanese 246th Battalion walloped the 43rd with good accuracy. Also a horde of Japanese planes were waiting for the Ken's Men before their Liberators reached target.

Col. Jim Pottys and Maj. Paul Hanson, who led the 43rd squadrons, warned their gunners to stay alert, to remain as calm as possible, and to expect heavy interception and dense anti-aircraft fire. The 43rd gunners responded, firing continually at attacking Japanese fighter planes. They downed three Oscars and damaged more. The Ken's Men, however, suffered damage to two Liberators and the loss of a third. A fourth plane, a 33rd Squadron B-24, had been so badly shot up by 20mm shells that the B-24 turned back from target area and crash landed at Batoedoka

Island, where a submarine rescued six crew members who had survived the crash. However, before the B-24 went down, the Ken's Men gunners aboard had shot down an astonishing six enemy fighter planes.

As the 43rd Bomb Group approached target, Jim Pottys called his squadron and flight leaders. "Keep the formation tight; keep it tight. If anybody goes down, the wingman will close in to retighten formation."

"Okay, Colonel," Maj. Paul Hanson answered.

Then, for the third time in the last 20 minutes, a lead bombardier carefully studied his target through a Norden bomb sight. And soon, he released the pathfinder flare and then yelled into his radio.

"Bombs away!"

A skyful of 500 pound demolition bombs tumbled out of the bellies of the B-24s and fell on the oil complex. Six bombs fell squarely on the already burning Edeleanu plant. Another bomb landed 25 feet from the power station, continued on through the full length of the pipes, and then exploded to tear apart the entire installation. Another 24 bombs exploded atop the Edeleanu plant and a half dozen large storage tanks, destroying whatever was left of the sulfuric acid structure and also destroying the storage tanks. One string of five demos near missed some smaller oil storage tanks, but ignited huge fires from burning oil. Only one incendiary and two demolition bombs missed completely and these bombs landed in the water beyond the oil complex. Finally, six bombs hit the boiler house to start fires.

As the Ken's Men arced away from target, they left in their wake a mass of wreckage. Smoke rose to

16,000 feet in the air and spirals could be seen up to 100 miles away.

While the 43rd Bomb Group droned away from Balikpapan, consternation reigned throughout the area. Japanese troops, Indonesian civilians, Chinese coolies, and General Ichabangese stared with horror at the rampant fires and smoke that enveloped the refineries. More than 100 Japanese soldiers and coolie workers had been killed in the oil complex, despite warnings to evacuate the area. No one on the ground could even see the Pandansari, Edeleanu, or power station areas because of the thick smoke, and no one could get near any of the plants because of blazing hot fires.

Meanwhile, in the sky, both the 381st Sentai and the 20th Kokutai had been badly decimated by the American fighter pilots and B-24 gunners. The Japanese had downed three Liberators and damaged 14 more, but they had only downed one fighter plane, the P-47 of Lt. Hilton Kessel. In return the two Japanese air units assigned to protect Balikpapan had lost 26 planes to American fighter pilots of the 41st and 40th Squadrons and 12 more planes to B-24 gunners, six to the B-24 the Japanese had shot down. Another 20 damaged planes from the 381st and 20th were forced to return to their Manggar and Samarinda airfields.

General Ichabangese, wearing a combat helmet and flak jacket for the first time, could not loiter on his luxurious headquarters balcony. Instead, the general moved about the Balikpapan area, avoiding the crackling fires of the oil complex, cringing from the echo of aircraft machine guns in the sky, and jerking from each new boom of ack ack fire. He soon found Maj. Toshiro Magari who was directing a pair of AA teams against the departing Ken's Men bombers.

"Major," Ichabangese cried. When Magari turned, the general glared at him. "Why have you allowed this to happen? Why? They are utterly destroying the refinery."

"We are doing our best, Honorable Ichabangese," Magari answered. "We have damaged many of the enemy bombers and we have shot down at least two of them."

"But you did not disrupt their accuracy by one iota, not one iota," the general wagged a finger angrily.

"We are not the only ones who failed," the major scowled. "What of the hordes of aircraft in the sky? Our interceptors have been falling like lotus blossoms against only half their number in enemy aircraft. Why did they not stop these interlopers?"

Ichabangese did not answer. Instead, his neck reddened further and he squinted upwards where hordes of fighter planes from both sides arced and darted about the sky. The Japanese pilots were seeking some way to deal with the Americans, while the U.S. pilots of the 41st and 40th Squadrons were loitering about to chase off the Japanese again as soon as the 13th Air Force Liberators came over target. Ichabangese stared for about two minutes at these planes and he then looked again at the fires and smoke that raged uncontrollably at the Balikpapan refineries. A moment later, an aide reached him.

"Please excuse the intrusion, Honorable General, but we have a new radar report. More Yankee bombers are coming across Balikpapan Bay to bombard the refineries."

"More?" Ichabangese gasped. "You mean they are not yet finished with this air attack?"

"Apparently not," the aide answered. "And worse, these new intruders also have fighter planes with them."

"And more fighter planes also?" The general barked.

"Yes, Honorable Ichabangese."

The Makassar Base Force commander wiped the perspiration from his face and he then turned to Toshiro Magari. "Major, you must double your effort. We have suffered enough damage to the refineries and we cannot afford more."

"We will do our utmost."

Ichabangese then looked at Colonel Kichi. "Send messengers to the headquarters of the 381st Sentai and 20th Kokutai. Tell whomever they find to contact Lieutenant Anabuki and Lt. Commander Fujita and order them to stop these new formations of American bombers." He shook his head. "I dread facing General Anami or Admiral Fuchida. They will be furious indeed when they learn what happened here. Only Heaven knows how much of the refinery is still functioning, and we must save whatever we can."

In fact, all that were left intact were the paraffin-lube plant, the cracking plant, and some of the storage tanks near the shoreline. These targets would become fair game for the Liberators of the 5th and 307th Bomb Groups whose planes were ringed by the P-38s of the 9th Headhunter Squadron. As the B-24s flew over Balikpapan with their escort, Wally Jordan called Charlie King.

"What's the opposition up ahead?"

"A horde of Nip fighters, but they're like fish in a barrel," King answered. "We're having a ball."

"Well Goddamn, Charlie," Jordan cried, "don't hog them all for yourself. Leave some for us."

"You'll find plenty, Wally, plenty," King said.

"I can't wait," Maj. Wallace Jordan answered.

Chapter Twelve

At 1120 hours, as Col. Tom Musgrave approached target, he could see the dense smoke and blazing fires that engulfed the Balikpapan refineries. He could also see an array of shipping in the harbor that offered good targets: at least four 500 ton Fox Tare supply ships and five small 300 ton Sugar Charlie supply ships. He also saw about fifty 200 ton barges, most of which carried oil. Musgrave would have liked to hit this shipping, but his target was the paraffin plant, which he had damaged in earlier raids.

The Bombers Baron colonel only caught glimpses of the plant because of the dense smoke over the area and Musgrave called Bombardier Fred Bonds. "Lieutenant, will you have trouble lining up the target?"

"I don't think so, sir."

"How long before we reach IP?"

"A couple of minutes, Colonel."

"Good," Musgrave said. The colonel then stared at the heavy puffs of exploding flak that were bursting all about his 5th Group formation. Major Toshiro Magari had apparently charged his 246th AA Battalion gunners to greater efforts. The Japanese were now throwing up anti aircraft shells at an intense pace. However, although AA shrapnel caused damage to some B-24's, the ack ack did not seriously damage any planes.

Gunner Harold Trout, on Musgrave's lead plane, ogled at the black puffs beyond his nose compartment and he winced with each new burst. Similarly, Gunners Jim Shaw in the tail section and Merv Anderson in the belly turret watched the exploding puffs of flak anxiously, jerking with each new concussion. They hoped that no interceptors jumped them to abet the thick anti aircraft fire. But the Japanese soon dispelled such hopes.

Despite the severe earlier punishment by American fighter pilots, both Lieutenant Anabuki and Lt. Commander Fujita rallied their pilots to assail the new swarm of U.S. heavy bombers. The ranks of the Japanese air units had been reduced by 50% or more, but still, the surviving Nippon pilots roared after the B-24s in a coordinated attack.

"Lieutenant, you and your pilots will attack the American bombers from the north at medium and high altitudes," Fujita told Satoshi Anabuki. "We will attack these intruders from the south at medium and low level."

"Yes, Commander," Anabuki answered. "I will have the six Kawasaki aircraft which carry phosphorous bombs fly atop the enemy bombers so they can drop these explosives from above."

But the pilots of the 20th Kokutai and 381st Sentai again ran into stiff resistance from American fighter pilots. Not only was Major Charlie King still loitering in the skies with his P-47s of the 41st and 40th Squadrons, but now, Major Wally Jordan and his P-38 Headhunters had arrived over Balikpapan. As soon as King noted the Japanese forming up to attack the Liberators, he called Jordan.

"Wally, it looks like the Nips intend to hit the Libs from a north and south direction. We'll take the Japanese planes to the south. Can your squadron take the Nip interceptors to the north?"

"A pleasure," Jordan answered.

Thus, before the Japanese pilots waded into the V's of droning Liberators, the American fighter pilots intervened. Wally Jordan cried into his intercom. "Drop tanks and attack. Hit them in pairs; in pairs!"

"I read you, Wally," Major Dick Bong said.

The pilots of the 9th Squadron then dropped their 315 gallon auxiliary tanks before a new dogfighter ensued north of the B-24 formation. The men aboard the Liberators watched in a mixture of curiosity and apprehension. They were eager to see how well the American fighter pilots dealt with the Japanese, and the Bomber Baron crews were treated to a joyful show.

From 15,000 feet, Jordan and his wingman from Blue Flight, Lt. Howes, roared after the V of Japanese planes heading for the Liberators. The two American pilots came down to 12,000 feet and opened with chattering .50 caliber fire and rocketing 37mm shells from 250 to 300 yards. Lt. Anabuki was shocked by the sudden onslaught. He saw his own plane get tattooed with fire, but luckily the damage was not serious. However, the 381st commander's two companions were not so fortunate.

Jordan had the sun behind him so that Anabuki's left wingman did not even see the American P-38. The Japanese pilot took no evasive action until he caught heavy .50 caliber hits from Jordan's forward guns. The Oscar pilot then made a slight turn left, but too late. The plane burned violently before flipping over, dropping quickly, and crashing into Balikpapan Bay. Anabuki's right wingman caught a burst of .50 caliber tracers in the cockpit from Lt. Howes' guns. The fire shattered the compartment and killed the pilot before the Oscar arced in the sky and fell to earth in a fiery crash.

"I'll be damned, Major," Lt. Howes said, "those guys from the 41st were right. There's a lot of game up here."

"Stay alert, Lieutenant," Jordan answered.

Next, Major Dick Bong with wingman Joe Baker, also from Blue Flight, dove on another trio of Japanese planes, Oscars which had also been heading toward the American bombers. However, from somewhere to the left, a Japanese pilot riddled Bong's wingman with 7.7 fire and Baker zoomed his P-38 up and away to avoid further damage. The major scowled but then raced after the trio of Oscars by himself.

Bong, one of the best fighter pilots who had ever donned a U.S. uniform, had already scored 30 victories in the SWPA. Despite his long layoff from combat, and his recent soft life back in the states, the major had not lost his touch. He dove on the enemy V with blazing .50 caliber wing fire and a half dozen thumping shells. Within seconds, he got one of the three Japanese planes. The Oscar caught a 37mm hit that set the plane afire. The Japanese plane then made a full 180 degree turn, but quickly lost altitude and plopped into the bay. Bong next got in position to attack a Zeke which was streaking westward. The Japanese plane made a full 360 degree turn, but then came into position for a perfect shot by Captain Joe Baker, who cried into his radio.

"I got him, Major, I got him; get out of the way!"

"Roger," Bong answered. The major pulled up and away and allowed his wingman to open with .50 caliber fire. Baker's shots tore the Oscar apart and the plane tumbled to earth, crashing just behind the burning refinery.

Dick Bong and Joe Baker climbed high, now joined by Capt. Harry Brown, Major Jordan, and Lieutenant Howes. A moment later, the P-38 pilots of the 9th Squadron came down on more trios of Japanese planes. The Americans revved their P-38's to a diving speed of 400 MPH. Jordan almost ran head on into a Zeke, too close to get off a good shot, and he could only veer off and away. But, Capt. Harry Brown found himself in a good position and the captain unleashed a burst of .50 caliber fire that set the Zeke ablaze before the Japanese plane rolled over on its back and crashed into Balikpapan Bay.

Meanwhile, Bong had found an errant Sally bomber flying north, apparently trying to get out of harm's way. The major pounced on the twin engine medium bomber, despite fire from the gunners who sent streams of 7.7 bullets outward. Bong blasted the plane with tracers from his own forward .50 caliber guns. He also hit the Sally with two accurate 37mm shells. The bomber simply fell apart from the heavy firepower and the blazing Sally arced downward and crashed into the sea, taking its four man crew to their deaths. Thus, Bong had scored his second kill in a matter of minutes.

Other 9th Squadron pilots had also scored heavily

against the Japanese 381st Squadron. The Head-hunters knocked down at least four more planes and damaged several more. Lt. Anabuki again had no choice but to call off his attack against the American bombers which were now approaching target.

Meanwhile, Major Charlie King and his 35th Group pilots had given Lt. Commander Nobuo Fujita little rest. The American airmen waded into the enemy fighter planes for the second time within the last half hour. King and his wingman caught a trio of Tonys and knocked one of them out of the sky, while they damaged the other two. Lt. Bob Johnson, who had already downed two Japanese planes in this continuing fight over Balikpapan, now dove into another trio of planes with his wingman. Johnson managed to damage two of the Japanese aircraft with streaming .50 caliber fire, but he could not splash any of them before the more manueverable Tonys arced away and out of trouble.

But, Lt. Jim Mugavero and Lt. Walt Sweeney did get a couple of additional kills. Mugavero caught a Tony just as the Japanese plane went into a steep turn. The 41st Squadron pilot caught the plane in the belly and ripped open the fuselage before the plane exploded in midair. Meanwhile, Lt. Walt Sweeney chased an Oscar for several miles and finally opened on the enemy plane from 400 yards. The .50 caliber tracers chopped off the tail before the plane dropped to earth like a huge rock. The Japanese pilot, apparently inexperienced, had obviously panicked. Instead of manuevering away from the heavy P-47, he had tried to outrun the Thunderbolt—a fatal mistake.

More 35th Group pilots also scored against the Japanese interceptor pilots, downing three more planes from Lt. Commander Fujita's 20th Kokutai before the commander called off his attack against the American B-24s.

Although the Bomber Barons and Long Rangers still faced intense anti aircraft fire, they did not face any harassment from Japanese fighter planes. At 1125 hours, Bombardier Fred Bonds, in the nose of the formation's lead A/C 595 of the 5th Bomb Group, pinpointed the paraffin plant target. He then loosened his yellow pathfinder flare and cried into his intercom.

"Bombs away!"

Five demolition bombs dropped out of Colonel Musgrave's bomber and struck squarely on the paraffin-lube plant. The explosions erupted at least three huge balls of fire before more smoke rose from the battered structure. Only seconds later, ten more 500 pounders, half demolition and half incendiary, also rained down on the paraffin plant from the lead V of 5th Group bombers. More explosions shattered and battered edifice before new balls of fire and smoke rose from the target.

Behind Musgrave came the other 21 planes from the Bomber Baron group, whose bombardiers unleashed their mixed bag of 500 pound demo and incendiary bombs. At least a half dozen struck the lube oil plant and sent whooshing fires and dense smoke rising skyward. The 5th Group bombardiers also smashed an array of installations in the paraffin plant complex: the east pump house, the west pump house, the wax presses, adjacent storage tanks, cooling installation reclining tanks, and storage tanks north of the agitator plant. More fires and smoke curled skyward.

"We knocked the place apart, Colonel," Lt. Jim Russell cried excitedly into his radio.

"There can't be a wall left standing," Lt. Ken Gutheil also crowed over his intercom.

"We did a thorough job this time, a complete job," Tom Musgrave answered. "But don't relax. We've still got ack ack around us and some of those Nips interceptors may break through our fighter screen."

"We read you, Colonel," Lieutenant Gutheil said.

"All gunners, stay alert," the 5th Group colonel said.

Excitement now reigned among the Bomber Baron crews. Aboard Musgrave's own plane, gunners Jim Shaw, Merv Anderson, and Harold Trout ogled at the conflagration left behind them. On Jim Russell's A/C 572, gunners Joe Tribble, Charlie Smith, and Hal Phillips stared in awe at the dense smoke and hot fires below. On Ken Gutheil's *Blackjack*, gunners Chuck Lee and Wes Barker peered in awe at the square of destruction the B-24s the Bomber Baron group had left in their wake.

The 24 5th Group B-24s had barely left target when the 25 Liberators of the 307th Group approached IP. Col. Bob Burnham peered at the utter chaos in the refinery complex and he half scowled. The four preceding heavy bomber groups had left his own cracking plant target quite obscured amidst the massive square of fire and smoke.

"What the hell are we going to do, Colonel?" Bombardier Wes Brown asked.

"Can you study your map and get an idea where the cracking plant might be?"

"Yes sir." A few seconds later, Brown called Burnham. "I think I got it, Colonel."

"Then drop your flare when ready," Burnham said. The 373rd and 371st Squadrons will hit the cracking plant and the other B-24s from our group will hit whatever they can find."

"Yes sir," Lt. Brown answered.

Musgrave then took the lead planes of the 372nd Squadron over the coast and a moment later, Wes Brown dropped a blue pathfinder flare before he cried into his radio. "Bombs away!"

Then, 15 bombs from the lead V of B-24s sailed down on what the Americans hoped was the cracking plant on which the complex depended for gasoline refinement. The subsequent explosions and erupting blue fire told Burnham that his bombardiers had scored well, despite the heavy smoke cover.

"There can't be a damn thing left in that plant, Colonel," Lt. Ron Covington said.

"No, I guess not," Burnham answered.

Meanwhile, the seven B-24s under Major Cliff Reese singled out whatever was left standing of the refinery complex. Long Ranger bombers dropped both demolition and incendiary bombs on the oil drum factory that held a large number of stored drums. Other bombs fell on the pipeline to totally rupture them, while some bombs fell on the water treatment plant, the warehouses, and even on a float plane base on the shoreline.

By the time the last of the FEAF heavy bombers had left target, nothing was left intact on the sprawling mile square refinery complex. As the 5th and 307th Group planes turned from Balikpapan for the long flight back to New Guinea, a dozen Oscar and Tony fighters made halfhearted passes at the B-24 formations, with none of the Japanese pilots coming within 300 yards of the bombers. So their 7.7 machine gun fire did not even dent the American B-24s. The 381st Sentai and 20th Kokutai pilots had obviously run out of steam as well as enthusiasm. In turn, the gunners aboard the Liberators fired back at the Japanese planes but, from 800 to 1,000 yards, the Americans could not score any telling hits against the interceptors.

"Jesus," Gunner Joe Tribble said to a fellow gunner, Charlie Smith, "those bastards are pretty squeamish now."

"Our fighter pilots gave 'em a good working over," Smith said, "and I guess those Nips are too drained to come close to us anymore."

By noon, the din over Balikpapan had ended: no more rattling machine gun fire, barking shells, thundering AA fire, or concussioning bombs. The waves of American bombers were gone as were the skitting, darting, arcing escorts from the 41st, 40th and 9th U.S. Fighter Squadrons. Surviving Oscars, Tonys, and Zeros of the 381st Sentai and 20th Kokutai began alighting on Manggar and Samarinda Fields. Luckily for the Japanese, the hordes of American bombers had not added the two runways to their list of targets for today.

Soon only continued fires and spiralling black smoke from the debacle at the refinery reminded soldiers and civilians in Balikpapan that a devastating attack and furious air battle had taken place over this beautiful city on Borneo's east coast.

On the return flight to New Guinea, the U.S. fighter planes hung around and above the Liberators like barnacles, waiting to pounce on any Japanese planes that came out of Kendari or Manado during the flight across Makassar Strait and then Tomini Gulf. Instead, as the American airmen crossed the Celebes, they met a horde of U.S. fighter planes from the 35th Group's 39th Squadron and the 8th Group's three squadrons to escort the heavies for the rest of the way. Now, more than 100 P-47s and P-38s were accompanying the B-24s back to New Guinea.

Japanese radar men and lookouts reported the huge formation of American planes droning eastward. However, when Commander Iwami of the 22nd Kokutai and Lieutenant Nakase of the 382nd Sentai learned that more than 100 American fighters were accompanying the B-24's, the two Japanese air commanders wisely decided not to attempt any interception. Iwami and Nakase might well draw the wrath of superiors for this failure, but the two air leaders preferred such reprimands to the possibility of losing most of their remaining planes and pilots to the horde of sharp American pilots in their superior Lightnings and Thunderbolts.

When the B-24s landed at Noemfoor late in the afternoon, they had cause for celebration. Of the 120 B-24s that had made the trip to Balikpapan, only three were lost and about six seriously damaged, with all of these disabled planes reaching Kornasoren Drome. Further, the five American bomber groups had only suffered about 20 airmen killed and another

12 wounded. The fighter squadrons had only lost three planes. Unfortunately, Lt. Hilton Kessel was never found again and presumed dead, but the pilots of the other two U.S. fighter planes had been plucked from Makassar Strait by a PBY.

In turn, the Americans had taken a heavy toll against the Japanese. Between the Celebes air units and the Balikpapan air units which had intercepted the American formations, the Japanese had lost 53 planes and suffered damage to 50 more. Not since the holocast at Rabaul on 2 November 1943 had the Japanese suffered so many casualties in aircraft and pilots on a single day in the SWPA. The 10 October foray had proven that new Japanese pilots had been too poorly and too hastily trained to cope with even B-24 gunners, must less American fighter pilots in their superior P-38s and P-47s. The task of stopping American air formations, even when such U.S. planes had been airborne for five or six hours, had not only become impossible, but quite disastrous.

Gen. St. Clair Streett was elated by the results of today's efforts and he planned at least one more raid on the refineries within the next few days. He received an added piece of good news when General McMullen informed the 13th Air Force commander that FEAF service technicians would install twin belly tanks on P-38s from the 475th Fighter Group within the next couple of days and these fighters could also make the long escort trip to Balikpapan.

"I'll use them," Streett said. "But, I want recon reports before we plan the next FO to that refinery."

Ironically, Streett would need to wait two days before he could make an evaluation of the damage at

Balikpapan. The Japanese needed about 48 hours to snuff out all fires and smoke before recon PBYs could get a good look at the refinery site on the afternoon of 12 October. The Catalina snooper results, however, were on Streett's desk at his ADVON headquarters in Noemfoor by the evening of 12 October.

The PBY visual and photograph observations were excellent because the long range Catalina had reached Borneo under clear skies. The pipelines running north from the refinery to the shoreline had been ruptured in two places. The pipelines south of the refinery were also ruptured. The boiler house and the water treatment plant had been totally destroyed. At least 27 buildings had been destroyed or damaged in the warehouse area and ship loading areas, along with five buildings destroyed in the float plane base. Three large 120' diameter oil storage tanks and nine smaller oil storage tanks had been wrecked, as were three large gasoline tanks.

Among the major facilities at the oil complex, the FEAF bombers had caused near total ruin. At the paraffin-lube oil area, the main building, the power-house, several small buildings, pump house, boiler house, cowling installation building, four distilling tanks, and the fracturing machinery had been totally wrecked. The paraffin facilities would be out of business for several months according to estimates.

The entire Edeleanu plant had been rendered non-operational. The No. 1 and No. 2 plants had been destroyed as had been the sulfuric dioxide plant. Also wrecked were the plant's power house, boiler house, sulfuric acid house, and two 120' diameter kerosene tanks. Also destroyed were 56 of the 74 coolie barracks, the main building of the oil drum factory, 75% of the stores in this main building, and the storage bins north of the main building.

Finally, the big Pandansari complex had suffered the worst damage yet. The chemical laboratory, cleaning house, and chemical treatment section were in utter ruin as was the main building itself. American analysts believed that the Japanese would need at least a couple of months to repair the plant before they could again distill aviation gasoline.

By the evening of 12 October 1944, Japanese brass had gathered around a conference table at the Makassar Base Force headquarters in Balikpapan. Adm. Mitsuo Fuchida, commander of the 4th Air Fleet, had flown down from Singapore, while both General Anami and Colonel Matsumae had flown down from Kudat, Borneo. Also, Capt. Kameo Sonokawa of the 23rd Air Flotilla had flown in from his headquarters at Kendari in the Celebes.

The Japanese VIPs had surveyed the wrecked refinery earlier in the day, studying the extensive damage and concluding that they would need a couple of weeks of round-the-clock work before they could even hope to get out a few thousand gallons of refined fuel from the complex that had been turning out more than 3,000,000 barrels of fuel oil and gasoline a year.

The heavy damage report had prompted Imperial Japanese Headquarters in Tokyo to send General Anami and Admiral Fuchida to Balikpapan to determine what could be done. Anami, obviously irate, opened the conference by berating Ichabangese, Matsumae, Sonokawa, and Magari for their failure to protect the vital oil complex from the awesome American air attacks.

"What can I say except that all of you who were responsible for defending the oil complex have failed in your duty," the 2nd Area Forces commander said. "Neither the fighter units in the Celebes nor those at Balikpapan hampered this horrible enemy air assault. I must also conclude that the anti-aircraft gunners were totally inept since they did not shoot down a single American bomber." He then scowled at Mitsuo Fuchida. "I must tell you, Admiral, that Imperial Headquarters is incensed as is General Yamashita in the Philippines. As commander of the 4th Air Fleet, it was your responsibility to prepare a proper air defense for the refinery. But it appears obvious that you and your staff were incapable of taking such measures."

"We did what was necessary, General," Fuchida defended himself, "and you cannot blame the 4th Air Fleet staff because subordinates did not do their duty." Fuchida then glared at Ichabangese. "You are the commander of the Makassar Base Force and you were accountable for directing defensive operations here."

"I did what I could, Honorable Fuchida," Ichabangese said nervously. "It is not my fault that Imperial Navy Headquarters sent me inferior fighter pilots and Imperial Japanese Army Headquarters sent me worthless army pilots and anti-aircraft gunners who could not hit the side of a mountain."

Fuchida did not respond, but Anami's face

reddened and he wagged his finger irritably at the Makassar Base Force commander. "No, the fault was yours because you could not inspire these combat men to make a maximum effort. But then, how could you?" he sneered at Ichabangese. "You have known nothing but a wartime life of ease here at Balikpapan, while other commanders fought furiously against our enemies. You were inept, good for nothing but enjoying leisurely comforts. How could we expect any combat leadership from you? In truth, the shame is mine. I should have relieved you of command at Balikpapan as soon as this crisis became apparent, and I should have appointed someone who could have spurred our fighting airmen and soldiers to a successful effort."

General Ichabangese did not respond to Anami's scathing condemnation.

"The damage is done, General," Fuchida told Anami, "and there is no sense in discussing who is at fault. We must now decide what to do next."

"I agree," Anami sighed. "Still, the incompetence here has caused an even more serious problem than the damage to the refineries. The Indonesians appear to have lost faith in the Greater Asia Co-prosperity Sphere as the result of the wanton destruction caused by the Americans, who bombed the refineries with seeming impunity. I saw the serious doubts on the faces of these civilians as I toured the city and its environs today. Not only must we repair the refineries, but we must also restore Indonesian confidence in the Imperial Japanese Forces."

"That will not be easy, General," Fuchida said.

"No," Anami conceded, "but we must try. Meanwhile, we must begin at once the task of repairing the refineries, while we take new defensive measures."

"I have been promised more air units by Imperial Headquarters," Fuchida said. "They will send another 100 fighter planes to Balikpapan to stop any further incursions by American bombers. I will also endeavor to strengthen the air complements in the Celebes." Then, Fuchida scowled at Sonakawa and Matsumae. "I am most distressed because the fighter commanders at Kendari and Manado made no effort to intercept the American air formations while these bombers returned to their bases in New Guinea."

"I was told by Commander Iwami that there were too many fighters accompanying them," Captain Sonokawa said, "and he did not have enough aircraft at Kendari to make an effective interception."

"Still, he should have made an effort," Fuchida said. Then he sighed. "As I said, I hope to reinforce both Commander Iwami's Kokutai and Lieutenant Nakase's Sentai. Then they will have no excuse, will they, Captain?"

"No, Honorable Fuchida," Sonokawa answered softly.

Anami now looked again at Ichabangese. "You are to enlist the aid of every able bodied man and woman in the Balikpapan area to repair the refineries, and you will begin at once. All available military and civilians will be used. Only the combat airmen and anti aircraft gunners will be exempt."

"Some Indonesians may be reluctant to work at this task," Ichabangese said.

"Are you not in authority here?" Anami barked. "Are you suggesting that you do not have the means to make them work?"

"Of course, General," the Makassar Base Force commander said.

"I have asked my aides to make a list of items that we need for repairs," Anami continued, "and they have done well. We will have all material here within a few weeks and some items will be rushed here from the Brunei oil installations on the west coast of Borneo. These items should be here by late tomorrow. By then, General Ichabangese, you should have cleared away all debris to begin repairs."

"Yes, Honorable Anami."

Anami then sighed. "I do not believe there is anything more to discuss. I ask all of you to spare nothing in doing what must be done. If all goes well, we can have the refineries back in operation soon."

But Gen. St. Clair Streett, the OTC of the U.S. air efforts against Balikpapan had no intentions of giving General Anami any respites.

Chapter Thirteen

By the evening of 13 October, tons of material had arrived at Balikpapan. Coolie laborers and Japanese soldiers quickly unloaded and stacked pipes, conduits, electrical cables, building materials, machinery, prefabricated storage tank segments, and other equipment in neat piles along the refinery complex. However, General Anami had overestimated his ability to get replacement material from the home islands. Imperial Japanese Headquarters told the 2nd Area Forces commander that he would need to wait at least a month before such equipment could reach Balikpapan from the home islands.

Still, the material from Brunei would enable Makassar Base Force to repair enough of the refinery to begin operating within a week and to pump out at least several thousand barrels of refined fuel and gasoline a day.

Adm. Mitsuo Fuchida was also disappointed. He could get no new aircraft and pilots for Balikpapan or the Celebes. General Tomoyuki Yamashita, CinC of all forces in the Philippines, had refused to send a single plane or flyer into the Dutch East Indies, insisting he needed every aircraft and airman he had to defend the Philippines. He claimed that Fuchida had ample air units in his own 4th Air Fleet command and Fuchida should draw from these air units in

Southeast Asia to replenish his depleted Sentai and Kokutais. Yamashita also suggested that Fuchida urge his pilots into more strenuous efforts if the Americans attempted to attack Balikpapan again.

Fuchida grumbled, but he sent about 50 planes and pilots to Balikpapan from his 4th Air Fleet. However, he sent no new pilots or aircraft to the airbases in the Celebes.

Meanwhile, on the evening of the 13th, U.S. commanders of the 5th and 13th Air Forces held briefings for new attacks on Balikpapan the next day. This time, the bombers would carry even heavier bombs, 1,000 pound general purpose explosives. If anything was still serviceable at the Balikpapan refineries, the 1,000 pounders would surely knock out such targets.

Meanwhile, General McMullen had installed the dual fuel tanks on the P-38s of both the 80th Squadron and 433rd Squadrons during the past two days. These air units then joined the 9th, 40th, and 41st Squadrons in flying into Morotai for staging to Borneo. The five squadrons of P-38s and P-47s would escort B-24s on the following day's mission.

Maj. Jay Robbins of the 80th Squadron and Maj. Tom McGuire of the 433rd Squadron were already well established air heroes, having scored 16 and 21 kills respectively in the SWPA war. The two aces and their pilots welcomed the chance to take on Japanese pilots over Balikpapan.

Thus, besides 49 Liberators from the 90th, 22nd, and 43rd Groups, and 49 B-24s from the 5th and 307th Groups, the American air assault would also include an escort of 32 P-47s and 48 P-38s. The bombers would be even better protected on this next mission than they had been during the 10 October raid. Major Charlie King would again bring in his P-47s first to sweep aside any Japanese interceptors, while the P-38 squadrons hung close to the B-24s to ward off any Japanese fighters which broke through the Thunderbolt screen to attack the Liberators.

Both U.S. bomber crews and fighter pilots at the multiple briefings of 13 October listened to the FO strategy with eager anticipation since the U.S. airmen had suffered only minimal losses on the 10 October raid. They were no longer fearful of this faraway target. In fact, gunners like Joe Tribble, Chuck Lee, Harold Trout, Joe Black, Ralph O'Brien, or Steve Novak even felt a reverse apprehension—the U.S. fighter pilots would not leave any Japanese planes in the air for these gunners to knock down.

For the 14 October mission, General Streett had not even assigned fighter units to escort the B-24s to the Celebes before the long range fighters met the Liberators. Instead, the 13th Air Force commander has sent out medium bombers to the Halmaheras and Ceram Islands for the past two days to put out of business the Japanese fields at Bitjoli and Amboina. His airmen had done an excellent job, rendering both bases untenable. Neither the 19th Kokutai at Bitjoli nor the Japanese air unit at Amboina could send up planes against the American bombers.

As usual, the B-24s took off from Kornasoren Drome on Noemfoor between 0200 and 0300 on the morning of 14 October. The fighter squadrons took off from Morotai Island at 0500 hours to meet the bombers over the Molucca Sea at 0700.

Just before dawn and shortly after the U.S. fighters had joined the B-24s, lookouts and radar men aboard the submarine I-176 again detected the American air formation flying westward. Once more a messenger carried the report to Captain Zenji Orita in the I-boat's control room.

"It appears, Captain, that the enemy formation now numbers nearly two hundred aircraft, with about half of them fighter planes," the radar man said.

Orita scowled. "The Americans have obviously found a way to fly their fighter planes more than 1,000 miles one way. This is regrettable news for our forces in the west. It means that more of the Indies' resources and installations will come within range of the enemy's fighter aircraft."

"The enemy will mount even more vicious air bombardments with such fighter cover," the subordinate said.

"Yes," the submarine captain nodded, glancing at the radar report in his hand. He then sighed. "No doubt these bombers are again flying to Balikpapan to attack the refineries, but it may be a useless flight. I am told that the oil complex is now little more than rubble."

"Yes, Captain."

"Still, you will notify the headquarters of the Manado and Kendari airbases that an enemy air flotilla is flying westward and should be over the Celebes in about an hour. You will also notify the Makassar Base Force in Balikpapan to expect this Yankee air armada over the east coast of Borneo at about 1000 hours."

"I will do so, Captain."

When the report from I-176 reached Kendari and Manado, neither Commander Iwami nor Lieutenant Nakase showed much enthusiasm. They, like their airmen, felt quite depressed by the severe beating adminstered to them by the American fighter pilots on 10 October. They had lost over 20 planes and suffered damage to as many more with little injury to the Americans. Neither the 22nd Kokutai nor the 382nd Sentai flyers were anxious to tangle with the Americans again over Tomini Gulf. Still, both air commanders recognized their obligations and they mounted aircraft to meet the intruders. However, Commander Iwami could only get 17 serviceable planes in the air, while Lt. Nakase could only take 23 Oscars and Zeros off his field at Manado. This time, the two air commanders coordinated their take offs so they would reach the American formations at the same time.

At 0600 hours, waist gunner Frank Guiterre aboard Maj. Vern Ekstrand's lead plane saw the dots in the distance and he called the 90th Group bomber leader at once. "Bandits! Bandits at three o'clock high!"

The major and Co-pilot Ed Cromwell stared from the cockpit window and squinted at the small shapes in the distance. Ekstrand was about to pick up his radio and call Wally Jordan of the 9th Fighter Squadron when he saw a dozen P-38s suddenly pull away from the 80th Squadron and peel off to the south.

"Nip interceptors must be coming from both directions," Cromwell said.

213

The major nodded and then spoke over his VHF channel. "Bandits at both three and nine o'clock," he told his crews. "Gunners, stay alert: pilots, tighten your formation."

The Jolly Roger gunners reacted quickly, but no Japanese planes came within combat range of the Liberators. The Japanese airmen never got near the American bombers. Major Wally Jordan, leading the Headhunters, waded into the Japanese 382nd Sentai pilots and within moments he and his 9th Squadron flyers knocked four of the Japanese planes out of the air with no losses to themselves. The Headhunters had also damaged eight more Japanese planes before Lt. Nakase called off the fight.

"They are too strong, too strong," the 382nd Sentai commander told his pilots. "We will return to base and notify Balikpapan to expect these enemy bombers and their escorts over Borneo in about three hours." Then, the surviving Japanese pilots flew off.

"Okay, it's over," Jordan said.

"Goddamn, Major," Lt. Ed Howes said, "if we go after them, we can knock down the rest of them."

"And we'd also run short of fuel," Jordan said. "Return to formation."

To the south of the B-24s, Maj. Jay Robbins and his P-38 pilots of the 80th Squadron had waded into the Japanese Oscars and Zeros under Commander Iwami. The 22nd Kokutai commander managed to damage one P-38 so badly he forced the American pilot to return to Morotai. Ensign Susumu Ishihara, meanwhile, caught a P-38 squarely with 20mm fire and shot down the plane. The American pilot bailed out and he was later rescued by a PBY. However, these victories were little comfort. Within several minutes, the 16 Lightning pilots completely macerated the 22nd Sentai.

In a matter of minutes, Iwami lost five planes and suffered damage to nine more, five of them quite serious. He had no choice but to break off the fight.

Major Robbins also refused to chase the Japanese south. He too was concerned with fuel consumption. Robbins might need to engage a horde of Japanese planes over Balikpapan and the U.S. squadron leader wanted enough gas in the tanks of his P-38s to make certain the Lightnings could make it home.

The Liberators continued on schedule, leaving the Celebes without further incidents. Then, as they crossed Makassar Strait, Major Vern Ekstrand saw the P-47s of the 41st and 40th Squadrons zoom forward to take on Japanese planes that might rise from the Balikpapan airfields to intercept the American bombers.

At 0950 hours, the air raid sirens once more wailed through the city of Balikpapan and the surrounding countryside. Airmen of the 381st Sentai and 20th Kokutai hurried to their aircraft to challenge the approaching U.S. planes, while gunners of the 246th AA Battalion raced to their gunpits. Meanwhile, civilians sped to shelters they had constructed after the first raid over Balikpapan on 29 September. The Indonesians now cursed the Japanese even more. They had labored long and hard during the past two days at the refineries, and now they expected the American bombers to surely destroy their endless hours of toil in a matter of minutes. The civilians no longer believed that the Japanese fighter pilots could stop the Americans from plastering the oil complex. They had seen the inept efforts of the 381st and 20th air units a few days ago against the P-47s and P-38s and they expected a reply of that debacle today.

The American fighter pilots did not disappoint the Indonesians. Maj. Charlie King saw the Zeros, Oscars, and Tonys taking off from Manggar and Samarinda Fields, and he quickly called his P-47 pilots.

"Bandits coming up to meet us. Attack in pairs! In pairs! Remember, don't get cute. Use your speed and climb to advantage."

"Roger, Major," Captain John Young said.

"We read you, sir," Lt. Bob Johnson answered.

Despite the lopsided defeat a few days ago, the Japanese pilots showed surprisingly strong inclinations to take on the American fighter pilots for a new toe-to-toe donnybrook. Lt. Cmdr. Nobuo Fujita and Lt. Satoshi Anabuki had apparently worked their pilots into a frenzy, exhorting them to a maximum effort. But as on the 10th of October, the clash today was another one sided fight. In a matter of minutes, Maj. Charlie King and his pilots of the 40th and 41st Squadrons shot down an astounding 19 enemy planes.

King and Wingman Bob Johnson tailed a trio of Oscars, loosening a heavy fusillade of .50 caliber machine gun fire and 37mm shells. The barrage chopped one Oscar to pieces, blew up a second, and knocked the wing off the third before the three Japanese pilots even knew what hit them.

"Major, we got ourselves another field day," Johnson cried into his radio, a wide grin on his face.

"Let's find some more, Bobby," King answered.

Meanwhile Lt. Jim Mugavero and Lt. Walt Sweeney also attacked a V of Japanese planes and struck the enemy with a stream of machine gun fire and streaking 37mm shells. The attack destroyed two of the Tonys, while the third miraculously wobbled away, despite an array of hits.

Capt. John Young and Lt. Bill Strand came down on a trio of Japanese planes and attacked them from three o'clock high. The streaming machine gun fire and thumping shells caught all three planes. One of the Japanese fighters arced downward with trailing, smoke before smashing into the sea. The second broke in half and fell like two descending rocks, while the third simply blew up.

And so the massacre continued. After the 19 kills and the loss of only one P-47 from the 7.7 guns of Lt. Satoshi Anabuki, King called off the fight. "Okay, we're pulling back."

"You've got to be kidding, Major," Captain John Young complained. "We can get all of them."

"And also use up too much fuel to get home," King answered. "Break off. Let the P-38s take on the rest of them."

"Okay," Young sighed in disappointment.

And the P-38s were just as successful. Major Wally Jordan with his Headhunter squadron, Major Jay Robbins with his 80th Squadron, and Major Tom McGuire with his 433rd Squadron waded into the battered formation of Japanese planes. Chattering machine gun fire, screaming engines, and darting shells echoed across the sky. Once more, the Japanese suffered disaster. Wally Jordan got a Zeke that blew apart from two well placed 37mm shell hits. Dick Bong got a Zeke when he chopped off the wing of the enemy plane with streaming fire for his third kill of the Balikpapan air campaign.

Newcomer Tom McGuire added to his kill score when he got an astonishing three victories in less than a minute. McGuire took his pilots of the 433rd Squadron high into the sky and then came down on a flock of Zeros that were attempting to soar above the B-24s so they could drop phosphorous bombs on the Liberators formations.

"Let's break them up!" McGuire cried.

Before McGuire and his pilots reached the Japanese planes, the enemy pilots had dropped 30 aerial bombs. Most of them went awry, but one of them hit a B-24 squarely, chopping off the nose before the big bomber fell to earth and exploded, killing all aboard. But then, the Satans Angels pilots of the 433rd Squadron ripped into the Japanese formation. McGuire knocked the engine off one Zero, tore the tail off a second, and shattered the cockpit and pilot of the third. All three Japanese planes tumbled into Balikpapan Bay. Other 433rd Squadron pilots knocked down at least five more of the planes carrying the phosphorous bombs and the other two Zekes scooted away.

By the time the American bombers came over target, the American fighter pilots had shot down an amazing 47 Japanese planes. Added to the 46 downed four days earlier, the 381st Sentai and 20th Kokutai at Balikpapan had been reduced to less than a third of their aircraft complements.

Now, uncontested by Japanese fighter planes, the B-24s droned over the already smashed Balikpapan refineries in wave after wave. First came the 20 heavy Liberators of the 90th Group, then the 17 B-24s of the 22nd, and then the 21 Liberators of the 43rd. Following the 5th Air Force units, 24 Liberators from the 5th Bomber Baron Group and 25 more from the 307th Long Ranger group also blasted the the target. For nearly 45 minutes, whistling 1,000 pound demolition bombs sailed down on the shattered one mile square area. The heavy bombers finished off anything that was still standing. Igniting fires destroyed more power systems and set aflame shoreline piers. But worse, the big 1,000 pounders destroyed most of the equipment and supplies that had recently arrived from Borneo's west coast to begin repairs on the refineries.

Once more, the B-24s left blazing fires and thick smoke that rose 6,000 feet into the air. As the Liberators turned from target, however, enemy interceptors that had broken through the U.S. fighter screen shot down a second B-24, this one from the 5th Bomb Group. But, the Liberator gunners quickly avenged the loss by downing nine of the intercepting planes.

Steve Novak of the 90th Group, gunner Chuck Lee of the 5th, and gunner Joe Black of the 307th all downed enemy planes to raise their kill scores in the Balikpapan bombing strikes to three, two, and the two enemy planes respectively. Meanwhile, gunner Ralph O'Brien aboard Don Forke's 307th Group B-24 downed two Zeros in succession for his second and third kills of the refinery air campaign.

Except for the two B-24s downed, only six men were wounded aboard the other planes and no one killed. Patrolling Catalinas rescued the pilot of the P-47 that had been shot down.

As the U.S. air formation flew back to New Guinea, no Japanese planes at Balikpapan chased after them and no enemy aircraft rose from Manado, Kendari, Bitjoli, or Amboina to intercept the American airmen. The Japanese air units had been hit too badly to any longer challenge the FEAF flyers. Both the U.S. fighter pilots and the U.S. B-24 crews received heroes' welcomes when they landed at Morotai and Noemfoor. They had been even more successful today against enemy interceptors than they had been on the 10 October strike.

The next day, PBY reconnaissance planes confirmed the awesome results of the bombing raids on the Balikpapan refineries. Not one of the more than a 100 buildings in the oil complex was undamaged. Nor a single storage tank, large or small, any longer held a gallon of crude petroleum, fuel oil, or gasoline. The complex had no power or electricity. Finally, the tons of supplies and equipment recently brought from their site at Brunei to repair the oil complex now lay in burned, twisted, blackened rubble. Observers guessed that the Japanese would need at least six months to restore the Balikpapan refineries to their former productive capacity.

General Douglas MacArthur personally congratulated Gen. St. Clair Streett and Gen. George Kenney for the thorough job on the Borneo oil complex. Within a week, the 307th, 5th, and 90th Bomb

Groups received well earned Distinguished Unit Citations for their efforts. The 9th Headhunter Squadron of the 49th Fighter Group and the 41st and 40th Squadrons of the 35th Fighter Group also received Distinguished Unit Citations for their achievements in the air campaign.

Individual medals came to FEAF airmen by the dozens. Tom Musgrave, Bob Burnham, Vern Ekstrand, and Charlie King all won Distinguished Service Crosses. Ken Gutheil, Jim Russell, Don Forke, Charlie Briggs, and Wally Jordan all won Silver Stars as did gunners Joe Black, Ralph O'Brien, Chuck Lee, and Steve Novak. Distinguished Flying Crosses went to Don Covington, Charlie Smith, Wally Jordan, Bob Johnson, Dick Bong and a host of others. Curiously, George Kenney reprimanded Bong while he pinned the medal on the major's chest—for going off on a dangerous mission against the FEAF commander's orders.

For the Japanese, the holocaust at Balikpapan had disheartened everyone from the chiefs of staff in Tokyo to the lowliest private in the Philippines who awaited the expected American invasion. And worst of all, the Indonesians had lost faith in Japan and they were unlikely to cooperate in the future. The civilians saw the devastating Balikpapan raids as the beginning of the end for the Greater Asia Co-prosperity Sphere.

As often happens after a defeat, heads rolled. Both Colonel Maseo Matsumae and Captain Kameo Sonokawa lost their commands of the 7th Air Division and the 23rd Air Flotilla respectively. Further, Imperial Japanese Headquarters relieved General

Shasho Ichabangese of his Makassar Base Force command and recalled him to Tokyo in disgrace, as if he could fight the air battles personally for the failing Japanese airmen. Imperial Headquarters, strangely, did not criticize Anami but they scolded Admiral Mitsuo Fuchida for allowing supposedly inept men like Masayuki Nakase or Joyotara Iwami to lead interceptor air units.

The last complaint, however, was utterly without merit. Iwami was one of the most dedicated and courageous commanders in the Japanese Navy Air Force. He had fought vigorously and without complaint for more than two years in the Pacific war and he simply could not meet the Americans on equal terms with inexperienced pilots and inferior aircraft.

Gen. St. Clair Streett carried out one more raid on Balikpapan on 18 October, sending out only the 5th and 307th Bomb Groups who had made the first raid. This time, the 347th Fighter Group of the 13th Air Force escorted the B-24s to target. However, the American found Balikpapan totally closed in by dense cloud covers when they reached Borneo and they bombed with H2X radar with unobserved results. In any case, little was left to destroy after the first four raids, especially the attacks of 10 and 14 October.

And, disappointedly, the eager U.S. fighter pilots of the 347th did not meet a single interceptor during the long flight to Balikpapan and back. During the earlier raids, the 5th Air Force fighter pilots and FEAF B-24 gunners had almost wiped out the five Japanese Sentais and Kokutais that had been assigned to protect the oil complex and the 4th Air Fleet simply had nothing left to send out after American planes.

On 20 October, 1944, the Americans landed on Leyte Island in the Philippines to begin the reconquest of those islands. Although the U.S. forces met stiff resistance, they did not face as formidable an adversary as might have been expected. Admiral Onishi of the 4th Base Air Force was forced into using Kamikaze suicide pilots because he did not have enough aviation gasoline to mount all of his aircraft in continual round trip assaults on the American invasion force.

Admiral Koga was hampered in his plan to attack the American beachhead in a three pronged naval assault. Two of his fleets were forced to burn crude petroleum in their ship boilers because they could not get enough refined fuel oil out of Balikpapan. The crude oil hampered the movement, efficiency, and speed of the Japanese warships, and most of the vessels became easy prey for American naval pilots in Philippine waters.

The Balikpapan refineries remained crippled for the rest of the war. The Japanese had wavered in their decision to rebuild the refineries, fearing they would only restructure a good target that the Americans could destroy again. So, only minimal refined fuel came from here again, with most of the Japanese fuel and gasoline needs coming from the Brunei oil complex on the west coast of Borneo. By the time the Japanese reorganized any semblance of fuel allocations out of Borneo again, the Americans were fully entrenched in the Philippines, with established air and sea bases in Cebu, Mindoro, and Palawan. The

Americans could now effectively cut the shipping lanes between the Dutch East Indies and the Japanese homelands. By early 1945, U.S. submarines, surface ships, or aircraft were sinking countless Japanese ships, especially tankers, which sailed between the Indies and Japan proper.

"They talk a lot about Ploesti," General Streett told reporters in 1945, "but the efforts against the Balik-papan refineries made the conquest of the Philippines a hell of a lot easier and certainly shortened the war in the Pacific."

Cmdr. Shisei Yasumoto of the 103rd Escort Air Squadron said after the war: "We could only give new flyers 30 hours of flight instruction because the destruction of Balikpapan oil complex had drastically cut our training plane fuel allotments. Of 750 training planes, we only had gasoline rations for 180 of them. So, by the spring of 1945, we had nothing but raw, inexperienced pilots to fight the Americans and we did not even have many of these. So, defeat became inevitable."

For the Indonesians, the American FEAF bombers had deftly left their beautiful city intact during the raids on the oil complex. The Australians captured the eastern areas of Borneo in May of 1945. They found the refinery wrecked and rusting, but they did not find a single building damaged in the tropical city of Balikpapan.

"The Yank airmen were certainly on target," an Australian officer said. "They knew exactly what to hit and what to leave alone. Their stratetic bombing tactics were uncannily accurate."

PARTICIPANTS

AMERICANS

General Douglas MacArthur - CinC of SWPA Allied Forces

General George C. Kenney, CinC of Far East Air Forces (FEAF)

General St. Clair Streett, Commander, 13th Air Force

General Ennis Whitehead, Commander, 5th Air Force

5th Bomb Group, Noemfoor Island, Colonel Thomas Musgrave
    394th Squadron - Major Al James
    72nd Squadron - Major James Pierce

307th Bomb Group, Noemfoor Island, Colonel Robert Burnham
    370th Squadron - Major Clifford Reese

90th Bomb Group, Biak Island, Colonel Edward Scott
    320th Squadron, Major Vernon Ekstrand
    319th Squadron, Major Charles Briggs

43rd Bomb Group, Biak Island, Colonel Jim Pottys

22nd Bomb Group, Biak Island, Colonel Richard Robinson

686th Night Radar Squadron, Hollandia, Lt. Colonel James Dunkell

35th Fighter Group, Owi Island, Colonel Edwin Doss
    41st Squadron, Major Charles King
    40th Squadron, Captain John Young

49th Fighter Group, Cape Sansapor, Colonel George Walker
    9th Squadron, Major Wallace Jordan

8th Fighter Group, 80th Squadron, Morotai Island,

Major Jay Robbins

475th Fighter Group, 433rd Squadron, Biak Island, Major Thomas McGuire

JAPANESE

General Soemu Anami - CinC of 2nd Area Forces, Kudat, Borneo

General Shosho Ichabangese, commander of Makassar Base Force, Balikpapan

    Colonel Koichi Kochi, Chief of Staff, Makassar Base Force

Admiral Mitsuo Fuchida, commander, 4th Air Fleet, Singapore

7th Air Division, Colonel Maseo Matsumae, Headquarters, Kudat, Borneo

    381st Sentai, Balikpapan, Lt. Satoshi Anabuki

    382nd Sentai, Manado, Celebes, Lieutenant Masayuki Nakase

    383rd Sentai, Babo, New Guinea

    384th Sentai, Amboina, Ceram Island

23rd Air Flotilla, Captain Kameo Sonokawa, Headquarters, Kendari, Celebes

    19th Kokutai, Bitjoli, Halmahera Island, Lt. Commander Kuniyoshi Tanaka

    20th Kokutai, Balikpapan, Lt. Commander Nobuo Fujita

    22nd Kokutai, Kendari, Celebes Island, Commander Yoyotara Iwami

246th AA Battalion, Balikpapan, Major Toshira Magari

9th Fleet, Tarakan, Borneo, Admiral Kuso Morita
Submarine I-176, Captain Zenji Orita

BIBLIOGRAPHY

Books

Alcorn, John, *The Jolly Rogers,* Historical Aviation Album Publishers, Temple City, Calif. 1973

Anders, Curt, *Fighting Airmen,* G.P. Putnam Publishers, New York City, 1966

Birdsall, Steve, *Log of the Liberators,* Doubleday & Co., New York City, 1963, *History of the 5th Air Force,* Doubleday & Co., New York City, 1963

Bowman, Martin, *The B-24 Liberator, 1939-1945,* Rand McNally & Co., New York City, 1979

Caidin, Martin, *Zero Fighter,* Ballantine Books, New York City, 1971

Crabb, J.V. General, *5th Air Force Against Japan,* USAF Publication, Washington, DC, 1946

Craven, Wesley, & Cate, James, *The AAF in World War II, Volume V, The Pacific: Matterhorn to Nagasaki,* Univ. of Chicago Press, Chicago, Ill., 1950

Dahm, Bernard, *History of Indonesia,* Chapter 4, "The Japanese Interregnum, 1942-1945," Praeger Publications, New York City, 1941

Greenfield, Kent, *The War Against Japan,* OCMH Department of the Army, Washington, DC, 1961

Hanna, William, *Bung Karno's Indonesia,* Chapter XIV, "The Bandung and Balikpapan Perspective," and Chapter 21, "The Japanese Pay Up," American University Field Staff Publication, New York City, 1961

Haugland, Vern, *The Army Air Force in World War II,* Harper & Bros., New York, 1948

Harrington, Joseph, *I-Boat Captain*, Major Books, Canoga Park, Calif. 1976

Hess, William, *Pacific Sweep*, Doubleday and Company, New York City, 1974

Legge, J.D., *Indonesia*, Prentiss-Hall Publisher, Englewood Cliffs, NJ, 1965

Maurer, Maurer, *Air Combat Units of World War II*, Department of the Air Force, Washington, DC, 1960

Rust, Ken, *5th Air Force Story*, Historical Aviation Album Publishers, Temple City, Calif, 1973

Sims, Edward, *American Aces*, Harper & Bros., New York City, 1958

Toliver, Raymond, & Constable, Trevor, *Fighter Aces of the USA*, Aero Publishers, Fallbrook, Calif., 1979

Ulonoff, Stanley M., *Fighter Pilot*, Doubleday & Company, New York City, 1962

Historical Record Sources:

All records are from the Alfred F. Simpson Hist Research Center archives, USAF, Air University, M. well AF Base, Alabama

Mission Reports:

    5th Bomb Group FO 153, 30 September 1944
    5th Bomb Group FO 155, 10 October 1944
    5th Bomb Group FO 158, 14 October 1944
    307th Bomb Group FO 307, 30 September 1944
    307th Bomb Group, FO 338, 3 October 1944
    307th Bomb Group, FO 347 10 October 1944
    90th Bomb Group, FO 284 A-1, 12 October 1944
    90th Bomb Group, 400th Squadron, FO 284 A-1, 12 October 1944

22nd Bomb Group, 2nd Squadron, FO 284, 10
    October 1944
22nd Bomb Group, 19th Squadron, FO 284, 10
    October 1944
9th Fighter Squadron, FO 330, 12 October 1944

Narrative Combat Reports:
    331st Squadron, 90th Bomb Group, 1 October
        1944
    319th Squadron, 90th Bomb Group, 1 October
        1944
    400th Squadron, 90th Bomb Group, 1 October
        1944
    90th Bomb Group History, October 1944
    43rd Bomb Group, FO 284 A-J, 14 October 1944
    41st Fighter Squadron, FO 284 A-K 10 October
        1944
    35th Fighter Group history, 1 January 1944 to 31
        December 1944
    90th Bomb Group History, September 1944

Daily Intelligence Summaries
    13th Air Force, period ending 1 October 1944
    13th Air Force, period ending 4 October 1944
    13th Air Force, period ending 11 October 1944
    XIII Bomber Command, 10 October 1944, Re-
        port #714, Balikpapan
    XIII Bomber Command, 14 October 1944, Re-
        port #184, Balikpapan
    XIII Air Force Reconnaissance Reports, 11
        October 1944

Japanese Sources:

Microfilm JD 1A, Planning a Defense of the Philippines

Microfilm JD 34, War Diary of Desron 11, 9th Fleet

USSBS (Interrogations of Japanese Officers)

#5 - Balikpapan Raids, 10 January 1946, pp 24-28

#6 - Oil In Japanese War, 1945, Report of Oil and Chemical Division

#66 - Rear Admiral K. Morita, 9 October 1945

#113 - 10 October 1945, Admiral M. Fuchida

#194 - Lt. Cmdr Shisei Yasumoto, 103rd Convoy Escort Squadron

#233 - Cmdr.Kokichi Mori - 9th Fleet Operations

#249 - Colonel M. Matsumae, 1 October 1945

#387 - Captain Kameo Sonokawa, 23rd Air Flotilla

#414 - Japanese Air Power - pp 20-28

#BPKI - Report from General Shosho Ichabangese

PHOTOGRAPHS:

All photos from National Archives and U.S. Air Force

MAPS:

All maps from U.S. Air Force, Simpson Research Center

ACKNOWLEDGEMENT: The author would like to thank the staff of the Alfred F. Simpson Historical Research Center for the cooperation in furnishing record information from their archive files. I am especially grateful to Mr. Carghill Hall, Director of Research, and his able assistants: Mr. Pressley Bickerstaff, Mrs. Margaret Claiborn, and Mrs. Judy Endicott.